BY MARGUERITE YOURCENAR

ORIENTAL TALES

TRANSLATED FROM THE FRENCH
BY ALBERTO MANGUEL
IN COLLABORATION
WITH THE AUTHOR
FARRAR STRAUS GIROUX
NEW YORK

MARGUERITE YOURCENAR

ORIENTAL TALES

Library of Congress Cataloging in Publication Data
Yourcenar, Marguerite.
Oriental tales.
Translation of: Nouvelles orientales.
Contents: How Wang-Fo was saved—Marko's smile—
The milk of death—[etc.]
1. Yourcenar, Marguerite—Translations, English.
2. East—Fiction.   I. Title.
PQ2649.O8N7413   1985   843'.912   85-12876

FOR ANDRÉ L. EMBIRICOS

CONTENTS

HOW WANG-FO

WAS SAVED

The old painter Wang-Fo and his disciple Ling were wandering along the roads of the Kingdom of Han.

They made slow progress because Wang-Fo would stop at night to watch the stars and during the day to observe the dragonflies. They carried hardly any luggage, because Wang-Fo loved the image of things and not the things themselves, and no object in the world seemed to him worth buying, except brushes, pots of lacquer and China ink, and rolls of silk and rice paper. They were poor, because Wang-Fo would exchange his paintings for a ration of boiled millet, and paid no attention to pieces of silver. Ling, his disciple, bent beneath the weight of a sack full of sketches, bowed his back with respect as if he were carrying the heavens' vault, because for Ling the sack was full of snow-covered mountains, torrents in spring, and the face of the summer moon.

Ling had not been born to trot down the roads, following an old man who seized the dawn and captured the dusk. His father had been a banker who dealt in gold, his mother the only child of a jade merchant who had left her all his worldly possessions, cursing her for not being a son. Ling had grown up in a house where wealth made him shy: he was afraid of insects, of thunder and the face of the dead. When Ling was fifteen, his father

chose a bride for him, a very beautiful one because
the thought of the happiness he was giving his son
consoled him for having reached the age in which
the night is meant for sleep. Ling's wife was as
frail as a reed, childish as milk, sweet as saliva, salty
as tears. After the wedding, Ling's parents became
discreet to the point of dying, and their son was
left alone in a house painted vermilion, in the company of his young wife who never stopped smiling
and a plum tree that blossomed every spring with
pale-pink flowers. Ling loved this woman of a
crystal-clear heart as one loves a mirror that will
never tarnish, or a talisman that will protect one
forever. He visited the teahouses to follow the dic-
tates of fashion, and only moderately favored acro-
bats and dancers.

One night, in the tavern, Wang-Fo shared Ling's
table. The old man had been drinking in order to
better paint a drunkard, and he cocked his head to
one side as if trying to measure the distance between his hand and his bowl. The rice wine undid
the tongue of the taciturn craftsman, and that
night Wang spoke as if silence were a wall and
words the colors with which to cover it. Thanks to
him, Ling got to know the beauty of the drunkards'
faces blurred by the vapors of hot drink, the brown
splendor of the roasts unevenly brushed by tongues
of fire, and the exquisite blush of wine stains strewn

on the tablecloths like withered petals. A gust of wind broke the window: the downpour entered the room. Wang-Fo leaned out to make Ling admire the livid zebra stripes of lightning, and Ling, spellbound, stopped being afraid of storms.

Ling paid the old painter's bill, and as Wang-Fo was both without money and without lodging, he humbly offered him a resting place. They walked away together; Ling held a lamp whose light projected unexpected fires in the puddles. That evening, Ling discovered with surprise that the walls of his house were not red, as he had always thought, but the color of an almost rotten orange. In the courtyard, Wang-Fo noticed the delicate shape of a bush to which no one had paid any attention until then, and compared it to a young woman letting down her hair to dry. In the passageway, he followed with delight the hesitant trail of an ant along the cracks in the wall, and Ling's horror of these creatures vanished into thin air. Realizing that Wang-Fo had just presented him with the gift of a new soul and a new vision of the world, Ling respectfully offered the old man the room in which his father and mother had died.

For many years now, Wang-Fo had dreamed of painting the portrait of a princess of olden days playing the lute under a willow. No woman was sufficiently unreal to be his model, but Ling would do because he was not a woman. Then Wang-Fo spoke of painting a young prince shooting an arrow at the foot of a large cedar tree. No young man of the present was sufficiently unreal to serve as his model, but Ling got his own wife to pose under the plum tree in the garden. Later on, Wang-Fo painted her in a fairy costume against the clouds of twilight, and the young woman wept because it was an omen of death. As Ling came to prefer the portraits painted by Wang-Fo to the young woman herself, her face began to fade, like a flower exposed to warm winds and summer rains. One morning, they found her hanging from the branches of the pink plum tree: the ends of the scarf that was strangling her floated in the wind, entangled with her hair. She looked even more delicate than usual, and as pure as the beauties celebrated by the poets of days gone by. Wang-Fo painted her one last time, because he loved the green hue that suffuses the face of the dead. His disciple Ling mixed the colors and the task needed such concentration that he forgot to shed tears.

One after the other, Ling sold his slaves, his jades, and the fish in his pond to buy his master pots of purple ink that came from the West. When the house was emptied, they left it, and Ling closed the door of his past behind him. Wang-Fo felt weary of a city where the faces could no longer teach him secrets of ugliness or beauty, and the master and his disciple walked away together down the roads of the Kingdom of Han.

Their reputation preceded them into the villages, to the gateway of fortresses, and into the atrium of temples where restless pilgrims halt at dusk. It was murmured that Wang-Fo had the power to bring his paintings to life by adding a last touch of color to their eyes. Farmers would come and beg him to paint a watchdog, and the lords would ask him for portraits of their best warriors. The priests honored Wang-Fo as a sage; the people feared him as a sorcerer. Wang enjoyed these differences of opinion which gave him the chance to study expressions of gratitude, fear, and veneration.

Ling begged for food, watched over his master's rest, and took advantage of the old man's raptures to massage his feet. With the first rays of the sun, when the old man was still asleep, Ling went in pursuit of timid landscapes hidden behind bunches of reeds. In the evening, when the master, disheartened, threw down his brushes, he would carefully pick them up. When Wang became sad and spoke of his old age, Ling would smile and show him the solid trunk of an old oak; when Wang felt happy and made jokes, Ling would humbly pretend to listen.

One day, at sunset, they reached the outskirts of

the Imperial City and Ling sought out and found an inn in which Wang-Fo could spend the night. The old man wrapped himself up in rags, and Ling lay down next to him to keep him warm because spring had only just begun and the floor of beaten earth was still frozen. At dawn, heavy steps echoed in the corridors of the inn; they heard the frightened whispers of the innkeeper and orders shouted in a foreign, barbaric tongue. Ling trembled, remembering that the night before, he had stolen a rice cake for his master's supper. Certain that they would come to take him to prison, he asked himself who would help Wang-Fo ford the next river on the following day.

The soldiers entered carrying lanterns. The flames gleaming through the motley paper cast red and blue lights on their leather helmets. The string of a bow quivered over their shoulders, and the fiercest among them suddenly let out a roar for no reason at all. A heavy hand fell on Wang-Fo's neck, and the painter could not help noticing that the soldiers' sleeves did not match the color of their coats.

Helped by his disciple, Wang-Fo followed the soldiers, stumbling along uneven roads. The passing crowds made fun of these two criminals who were certainly going to be beheaded. The soldiers answered Wang's questions with savage scowls. His bound hands hurt him, and Ling in despair looked smiling at his master, which for him was a gentler way of crying.

They reached the threshold of the Imperial Palace, whose purple walls rose in broad daylight like a sweep of sunset. The soldiers led Wang-Fo through countless square and circular rooms whose shapes symbolized the seasons, the cardinal points, the male and the female, longevity, and the prerogatives of power. The doors swung on their hinges with a musical note, and were placed in such a manner that one followed the entire scale when crossing the palace from east to west. Everything combined to give an impression of superhuman power and subtlety, and one could feel that here the simplest orders were as final and as terrible as the wisdom of the ancients. At last, the air became thin and the silence so deep that not even a man under torture would have dared to scream. A eunuch lifted a tapestry; the soldiers began to tremble like women, and the small troop entered the chamber in which the Son of Heaven sat on a high throne.

It was a room without walls, held up by thick columns of blue stone. A garden spread out on the far side of the marble shafts, and each and every flower blooming in the greenery belonged to a rare species brought here from across the oceans. But none of them had any perfume, so that the Celestial Dragon's meditations would not be troubled by fine smells. Out of respect for the silence in which his thoughts evolved, no bird had been allowed within the enclosure, and even the bees had been driven away. An enormous wall separated the garden from the rest of the world, so that the wind that sweeps over dead dogs and corpses on the battlefield would not dare brush the Emperor's sleeve.

The Celestial Master sat on a throne of jade, and his hands were wrinkled like those of an old man, though he had scarcely reached the age of twenty. His robe was blue to symbolize winter, and green to remind one of spring. His face was beautiful but blank, like a looking glass placed too high, reflecting nothing except the stars and the immutable heavens. To his right stood his Minister of Perfect Pleasures, and to his left his Counselor of Just Torments. Because his courtiers, lined along the base of the columns, always lent a keen ear to the slightest sound from his lips, he had adopted the habit of speaking in a low voice.

"Celestial Dragon," said Wang-Fo, bowing low, "I am old, I am poor, I am weak. You are like summer; I am like winter. You have Ten Thousand Lives; I have but one, and it is near its close. What have I done to you? My hands have been tied, these hands that never harmed you."

"You ask what you have done to me, old Wang-Fo?" said the Emperor.

His voice was so melodious that it made one want to cry. He raised his right hand, to which the reflections from the jade pavement gave a pale sea-green hue like that of an underwater plant, and Wang-Fo marveled at the length of those thin fingers, and hunted among his memories to discover whether he had not at some time painted a mediocre portrait of either the Emperor or one of his ancestors that would now merit a sentence of death. But it seemed unlikely because Wang-Fo had not been an assiduous visitor at the Imperial Court. He preferred the farmers' huts or, in the cities, the courtesans' quarters and the taverns along the harbor where the dockers liked to quarrel.

"You ask me what it is you have done, old Wang-Fo?" repeated the Emperor, inclining his slender neck toward the old man waiting attentively. "I will tell you. But, as another man's poison cannot enter our veins except through our nine openings, in order to show you your offenses I must take you with me down the corridors of my memory and tell you the story of my life. My father had assembled a collection of your work and hidden it in the most secret chamber in the palace, because he judged that the people in your paintings should be concealed from the world since they cannot lower their eyes in the presence of profane viewers. It was in those same rooms that I was brought up, old Wang-Fo, surrounded by solitude. To prevent my innocence from being sullied by other human souls, the restless crowd of my future subjects had been driven away from me, and no one was allowed to pass my threshold, for fear that his or her shadow would stretch out and touch me. The few aged servants that were placed in my service showed themselves as little as possible; the hours turned in circles; the colors of your paintings bloomed in the first hours of the morning and grew pale at dusk. At night, when I was unable to sleep, I gazed at them, and for nearly ten years I gazed at them every night. During the day, sitting on a carpet whose design I knew by heart, I dreamed of the joys the future had in store for me. I imagined the world, with the Kingdom of Han at the center, to be like the flat palm of my hand crossed by the fatal lines of the Five Rivers. Around it lay the sea in which monsters are born, and farther away the mountains that hold up the heavens. And to help me visualize these things I used your paintings. You made me believe that the sea looked like the vast sheet of water spread across your scrolls, so blue that if a stone were to fall into it, it would become a sapphire; that women opened and closed like flowers, like the creatures that come forward, pushed by the wind, along the paths of your painted gardens; and that the young, slim-waisted warriors who mount guard in the fortresses along the frontier were themselves like arrows that could pierce my heart. At sixteen I saw the doors that separated me from the world open once again; I climbed onto the balcony of my palace to look at the clouds, but they were far less beautiful than those in your sunsets. I ordered my litter; bounced along roads on which I had not foreseen either mud or stones, I traveled across the provinces of the Empire without ever finding your gardens full of women like fireflies, or a woman whose body was in itself a garden. The pebbles on the beach spoiled my taste for oceans; the blood of the tortured is less red than the pomegranates in your paintings; the village vermin prevented me from seeing the beauty of the rice fields; the flesh of mortal women disgusted me like the dead meat hanging from the butcher's hook, and the coarse laughter of my soldiers made me sick. You lied, Wang-Fo, you old impostor. The world is nothing but a mass of muddled colors thrown into the void by an insane painter, and smudged by our tears. The Kingdom of Han is not the most beautiful of kingdoms, and I am not the Emperor. The only empire which is worth reigning over is that which you alone can enter, old Wang, by the road of One Thousand Curves and Ten

Thousand Colors. You alone reign peacefully over mountains covered in snow that cannot melt, and over fields of daffodils that cannot die. And that is why, Wang-Fo, I have conceived a punishment for you, for you whose enchantment has filled me with disgust at everything I own, and with desire for everything I shall never possess. And in order to lock you up in the only cell from which there is no escape, I have decided to have your eyes burned out, because your eyes, Wang-Fo, are the two magic gates that open onto your kingdom. And as your hands are the two roads of ten forking paths that lead to the heart of your kingdom, I have decided to have your hands cut off. Have you understood, old Wang-Fo?"

Hearing the sentence, Ling, the disciple, tore from his belt an old knife and leaped toward the Emperor. Two guards immediately seized him. The Son of Heaven smiled and added, with a sigh: "And I also hate you, old Wang-Fo, because you have known how to make yourself beloved. Kill that dog."

Ling jumped to one side so that his blood would not stain his master's robe. One of the soldiers lifted his sword and Ling's head fell from his neck like a cut flower. The servants carried away the remains, and Wang-Fo, in despair, admired the beautiful scarlet stain that his disciple's blood made on the green stone floor.

The Emperor made a sign and two eunuchs wiped Wang's eyes.

"Listen, old Wang-Fo," said the Emperor, "and dry your tears, because this is not the time to weep. Your eyes must be clear so that the little light that is left to them is not clouded by your weeping. Because it is not only the grudge I bear you that makes me desire your death; it is not only the cruelty in my heart that makes me want to see you suffer. I have other plans, old Wang-Fo. I possess among your works a remarkable painting in which the mountains, the river estuary, and the sea reflect each other, on a very small scale certainly, but with a clarity that surpasses the real landscapes themselves, like objects reflected on the walls of a metal sphere. But that painting is unfinished, Wang-Fo; your masterpiece is but a sketch. No doubt, when you began your work, sitting in a solitary valley, you noticed a passing bird, or a child running after the bird. And the bird's beak or the child's cheeks made you forget the blue eyelids of the sea. You never finished the frills of the water's cloak, or the seaweed hair of the rocks. Wang-Fo, I want you to use the few hours of light that are left to you to finish this painting, which will thus contain the final secrets amassed during your long life. I know that your hands, about to fall, will not tremble on the silken cloth, and infinity will enter your work through those unhappy cuts. I know that your eyes, about to be put out, will discover bearings far beyond all human senses. This is my plan, old Wang-Fo, and I can force you to fulfill it. If you refuse, before blinding you, I will have all your paintings burned, and you will be like a father whose children are slaughtered and all hopes of posterity extinguished. However, believe, if you wish, that this last order stems from nothing but my kindness, because I know that the silken scroll is the only mistress you ever deigned to touch. And to offer you brushes, paints, and inks to occupy your last hours is like offering the favors of a harlot to a man condemned to death."

Upon a sign from the Emperor's little finger, two eunuchs respectfully brought forward the unfinished scroll on which Wang-Fo had outlined the image of the sea and the sky. Wang-Fo dried his tears and smiled, because that small sketch reminded him of his youth. Everything in it spoke of a fresh new spirit which Wang-Fo could no longer claim as his, and yet something was missing from it, because when Wang had painted it he had not yet looked long enough at the mountains or at the rocks bathing their naked flanks in the sea, and he had not yet penetrated deep enough into the sadness of the evening twilight. Wang-Fo selected one of the brushes which a slave held ready for him and began spreading wide strokes of blue onto the unfinished sea. A eunuch crouched by his feet, mixing the colors; he carried out his task with little skill, and more than ever Wang-Fo lamented the loss of his disciple Ling.

Wang began by adding a touch of pink to the tip of the wing of a cloud perched on a mountain. Then he painted onto the surface of the sea a few small lines that deepened the perfect feeling of calm. The jade floor became increasingly damp, but Wang-Fo, absorbed as he was in his painting, did not seem to notice that he was working with his feet in water.

The fragile rowboat grew under the strokes of the painter's brush and now occupied the entire foreground of the silken scroll. The rhythmic sound of the oars rose suddenly in the distance, quick and eager like the beating of wings. The sound came nearer, gently filling the whole room, then ceased, and a few trembling drops appeared on the boatman's oars. The red iron intended for Wang's eyes lay extinguished on the executioner's coals. The courtiers, motionless as etiquette required, stood in water up to their shoulders, trying to lift themselves onto the tips of their toes. The water finally reached the level of the imperial heart. The silence was so deep one could have heard a tear drop.

It was Ling. He wore his everyday robe, and his right sleeve still had a hole that he had not had time to mend that morning before the soldiers' arrival. But around his neck was tied a strange red scarf.

Wang-Fo said to him softly, while he continued painting, "I thought you were dead."

"You being alive," said Ling respectfully, "how could I have died?"

And he helped his master into the boat. The jade ceiling reflected itself in the water, so that Ling seemed to be inside a cave. The pigtails of submerged courtiers rippled up toward the surface like snakes, and the pale head of the Emperor floated like a lotus.

"Look at them," said Wang-Fo sadly. "These wretches will die, if they are not dead already. I never thought there was enough water in the sea to drown an Emperor. What are we to do?"

"Master, have no fear," murmured the disciple. "They will soon be dry again and will not even remember that their sleeves were ever wet. Only the Emperor will keep in his heart a little of the bitterness of the sea. These people are not the kind to lose themselves inside a painting."

And he added: "The sea is calm, the wind high,

the seabirds fly to their nests. Let us leave, Master, and sail to the land beyond the waves."

"Let us leave," said the old painter.

Wang-Fo took hold of the helm, and Ling bent over the oars. The sound of rowing filled the room again, strong and steady like the beating of a heart. The level of the water dropped unnoticed around the large vertical rocks that became columns once more. Soon only a few puddles glistened in the hollows of the jade floor. The courtiers' robes were dry, but a few wisps of foam still clung to the hem of the Emperor's cloak.

The painting finished by Wang-Fo was leaning against a tapestry. A rowboat occupied the entire foreground. It drifted away little by little, leaving behind it a thin wake that smoothed out into the quiet sea. One could no longer make out the faces of the two men sitting in the boat, but one could still see Ling's red scarf and Wang-Fo's beard waving in the breeze.

The beating of the oars grew fainter, then ceased, blotted out by the distance. The Emperor, leaning forward, a hand above his eyes, watched Wang's boat sail away till it was nothing but an imperceptible dot in the paleness of the twilight. A golden mist rose and spread over the water. Finally the boat veered around a rock that stood at the gateway to the ocean; the shadow of a cliff fell across it; its wake disappeared from the deserted surface, and the painter Wang-Fo and his disciple Ling vanished forever on the jade-blue sea that Wang-Fo had just created.

MARKO'S SMILE

The liner floated softly on the smooth waters, like a drifting jellyfish. With the unbearable buzzing of an angry insect, an airplane drew circles inside the narrow pane of sky framed between the mountains. Barely a third of a beautiful summer afternoon had gone by and already the sun had disappeared behind the barren buttresses of the Montenegro Alps peppered with thin trees. The open sea, so blue in the mornings, took on deeper shades inside that long, winding fjord cut mysteriously into the Balkan coast. The humble hunched-up houses, the healthy openness of the landscape were Slavic, but the dull violence of the colors, the naked arrogance of the sky, hinted at the Orient and Islam. Most of the passengers had disembarked and were trying to make themselves understood by the customs men dressed in white and by the wonderful soldiers armed with triangular daggers, each one as handsome as the heavenly warrior, Saint Michael. The Greek archaeologist, the Egyptian pasha, and the French engineer had stayed on board on the upper deck. The engineer had ordered himself a beer, the pasha drank whiskey, and the archaeologist lemonade.

"This country excites me," the engineer was saying. "The ports of Kotor and Ragusa are truly the only Mediterranean outlets of this vast Slavic land which spreads from the Balkans to the Urals, a region that ignores the changing frontiers on the map of Europe and boldly turns its back on the sea. The sea, in turn, does not enter it except through the intricate inlets of the Caspian, the Gulf of Bothnia, the Euxine, and the Dalmatian coast. And within that large human continent, even the infinite variety of races cannot destroy the mysterious unity of the whole, any more than the diversity of the waves can break the majestic monotony of the sea. However, at present my interest lies neither in geography nor in history, but in Kotor itself. The mouths of Cattaro, as they call it . . . Kotor, as we see it from the deck of this Italian liner, Kotor the wild, the hidden, with its zigzag road climbing toward Cetinje, and also the only slightly harsher Kotor of Serbian legends and epic poems. Kotor the infidel, once under the yoke of the Muslims of Albania, who are not always fairly treated in these poems—as you, Pasha, will certainly understand. But you, Loukiadis, you who know the past as a farmer knows every nook and cranny of his farm, are you going to tell me you have never heard of Marko Kraljević?"

"I'm an archaeologist," answered the Greek, putting down his lemonade. "My knowledge is limited to the chiseled stone, and your Serbian heroes prefer to chisel the living flesh. And yet Marko has stirred my interest too, and I have found his tracks in a country far from the birthplace of his legend, on purely Greek soil, even though Serbian piety has built there a number of rather lovely monasteries . . ."

"On Mount Athos," the engineer interrupted. "The giant bones of Marko Kraljević have found their resting place somewhere in that Holy Mountain where nothing has changed since the Middle Ages, except perhaps the quality of the souls, and where six thousand monks, their hair in a coil and their beards floating in the wind, pray even today for the salvation of their pious protectors, the Princes of Trebizond, whose line has been extinct for centuries. How comforting it is to think that oblivion is less prompt, less complete than one supposes, and that there is still a corner of the world where a dynasty dating from the Crusades survives in the prayers of a few old priests! Unless I am much mistaken, Marko died in a battle against the Ottomans, in Bosnia or some other Croatian country, but his dying wish was to be buried in this Sinai of the Orthodox world, and a small boat managed to carry his body there, in spite of the reefs of the Eastern sea and the ambushing Turkish galleys. A fine story which reminds me, I don't know why, of King Arthur's last crossing . . .

"There are heroes in the West, but they seem to be held up by the armor of their principles, much as the knights of the Middle Ages are by their iron shells. In this savage Serb, we see a hero stripped bare. The Turks against whom Marko launched his attack must have felt that a mountain oak was crashing down on them. I have told you that in those days Montenegro belonged to Islam: the Serbian hordes were not numerous enough to fight openly against the circumcised Muslims over Crna Gora, the Black Mountain, from which the country takes its name. Marko Kraljević had secret contacts among the infidels—falsely converted Christians, dissatisfied officials, pashas in danger of dishonor and death—and it became increasingly necessary to speak directly to his accomplices. But his height made it impossible for him to infiltrate the enemy ranks disguised as a beggar, as a blind musician, or as a woman, even though his comeliness would have permitted the latter: he would have been recognized by the immoderate length of his shadow. It was also unthinkable to moor a rowboat in a deserted spot along the coast: innumerable guards posted along the cliffs confronted a single and absent Marko with their multiple and tireless presence. However, where a boat can be seen, a good swimmer may remain invisible, and only the fish know of his trail in the water. Marko charmed the waves; he was as good a swimmer as Ulysses, his ancient neighbor from Ithaca. He also

charmed the women: the complicated fairways of
the sea led him often to Kotor, to the foot of a
wooden worm-eaten house that seemed to gasp under the thrust of the waves. There the Pasha of
Scutari's widow spent her nights dreaming of Marko
and her mornings waiting for him. She would rub
oil into his body frozen by the soft kisses of the sea;
she would warm him in bed unseen by her servants;
she would help him in his nocturnal meetings with
his agents and accomplices. In the small hours of
the morning, she would creep down to the still
empty kitchen and prepare for him the dishes he
loved best. He resigned himself to her heavy breasts,
to her thick legs, to her eyebrows that met in the
middle of her forehead, to the voracious and suspicious love of an older woman; he would swallow
his anger seeing her spit when he knelt down to
make the sign of the cross. On the eve of the day
on which Marko had decided to swim across to
Ragusa, the widow crept down, as she always did,
to prepare his meal. The tears prevented her from
cooking with as much care as usual; by misfortune,
she carried up a dish of overcooked kid. Marko had
been drinking; his patience had sunk to the bottom
of the jug.

"He grabbed her by the hair with grease-stained
hands and roared: 'You hell-hag, are you trying to
make me eat a hundred-year-old goat?'

" 'It was a fine animal,' the widow answered. 'The youngest in the herd.'

" 'It was as tough as your own hide, you witch, and had the same damn stench,' snarled the young Christian, drunk. 'May you boil like it in hell!' And with a kick he sent the dish out of the open window, which overlooked the sea.

"The widow silently washed the floor spotted with fat, and then her own face swollen with tears. She appeared to be neither less tender nor less warm than the day before; and at daybreak, when the north wind began to stir up the waves in the bay, she softly advised Marko to delay his departure. He agreed, and during the hot noon hours he lay down again for a nap. Upon waking, as he stretched lazily in front of the windows, protected by intricate blinds from the sight of the passersby, he saw in a flash the glimmer of scimitars: a troop of Turkish soldiers was surrounding the house, blocking all exits. Marko ran out to the balcony that hung high above the sea: the leaping waves crashed against the rocks with the sound of thunder in the sky. Marko tore off his shirt and dove headfirst into that tempest upon which no ship would have ventured. Mountains rolled under him, and he rolled underneath the mountains. The soldiers, led by the widow, ransacked the house without finding the slightest trace of the vanished young giant; finally the torn shirt and the broken railings of the balcony put them on the right track. They ran down to the beach, howling with vexation and terror. Every time a wave crashed with increasing fury at their feet, they drew back in spite of themselves. The gusts of wind seemed to them Marko's laughter, and the insolent foam his spit in their faces. For two hours Marko swam, unable to advance a single stroke; his enemies aimed at his head, but the wind turned their arrows aside. He would disappear, then appear again under the same green millstone. Finally the widow solidly knotted her scarf to the long lithe belt of an Albanian soldier; a clever tuna fisher managed to capture Marko with this silken lasso, and the swimmer, half strangled, had to allow himself to be dragged out onto the beach. Riding with the hunt in the mountains of his country, Marko had often seen animals play dead to avoid being killed; his instinct led him to imitate the ploy. The pale-faced young man the Turks carried onto the beach lay stiff and cold as a three-day-old corpse; his hair, speckled by the foam, stuck to his sunken temples; his fixed eyes no longer reflected the vast sky and the evening; his lips salted by the sea froze on his clenched jaws; his forsaken arms hung lifeless; and the bulk of his chest deadened the beating of his heart.

"The village elders leaned over Marko, tickling

his face with their long beards; then, lifting their heads, they cried in one breath: 'Allah! He's as dead as a rotten mole, as a slaughtered dog. Let us throw him back into the sea, the sea that washes away all worthless debris, so that our land may not be soiled by his corpse.'

"But the wicked widow began to cry, then laugh. 'You need more than a storm to drown Marko,' she said, 'and more than one knot to strangle him. In spite of what you see, he isn't dead. If you throw him into the sea, he will charm the waves as he charmed me, poor woman, and they will carry him back to his own country. Take a hammer and nails; crucify the dog as his god was crucified, his god who will not come to his help, and you will see if his knees do not twist in pain, if his cursed mouth does not vomit out cries.'

"The executioners took a hammer and nails from a ship carpenter's bench, pierced the hands of the young Serb, and drove a nail into his feet. But the tortured man's body remained motionless: no trembling crossed his seemingly senseless face, and even blood did not gush from the open wounds except for a few sluggish drops, because Marko was the master of his veins as he was the master of his heart.

"Then the oldest villager flung the hammer away and cried out in sorrow: 'May Allah forgive us for having tried to crucify a dead man! Let us tie a large stone to the neck of this corpse so that the abyss may not reveal our error or the sea bring him back to us.'

" 'You need more than a thousand nails and a hundred hammers to crucify Marko Kraljević,' said the evil widow. 'Take live coals and lay them on his chest, and you will see whether he does not squirm in pain like a large naked worm.'

"The executioners took burning coals out of a caulker's oven and drew a big circle on the chest of the swimmer chilled by the sea. The coals burned, then died out and became as black as dying red roses. The fire cut upon Marko's chest a large charcoal ring, like the rings made in the grass by dancing witches, but the young man did not moan, and not a single one of his eyelashes trembled.

" 'Allah,' said his executioners, 'we have sinned, for only God has the right to torture the dead. His nephews and his uncles' sons will demand an explanation for this outrage; let us hide him in a sack half full of heavy stones, so that the sea itself may not know whose body we are feeding it.'

" 'Unfortunate wretches,' said the widow. 'He will rip the cloth with his arm and toss out the stones. Instead, bring forth the young girls from the village and order them to dance in the sand, and we shall see whether love continues to torment him.'

"The young girls were called; quickly they put on their best outfits; they brought tambourines and flutes; they held hands to dance in circles around the corpse, and the loveliest of all, with a red scarf in her hand, led the dance. She was one dusky head and a white neck taller than the others; she skipped like a she-goat and flew like a falcon. Marko, motionless, let himself be brushed by her naked feet, but his restless heart was beating with ever-increasing violence and confusion, so loudly he feared that every one of the spectators would end by hearing it; and, in spite of himself, a smile of almost painful happiness began to draw itself on his lips, which were fluttering as if about to kiss. Thanks to the slow shadows of dusk, the executioners and the widow had not yet noticed this sign of life, but the clear eyes of Haiše were glued to the young man's face, because she thought him beautiful.

"Suddenly she let her red scarf fall to hide the smile, and said in a haughty voice: 'It is improper to dance in front of the naked face of a dead Christian; that is why I have covered his mouth, whose very sight filled me with horror.'

"And she went on dancing so that the executioners' attention would be diverted, as the hour of prayer was drawing near and they would be forced to leave the shore. Finally, a voice from high on a minaret cried out that the time to praise

God had arrived. The men walked away toward the rustic mosque; the tired girls trailed away toward the village in their heel-less slippers; Haiše left, turning her head many times; only the widow remained to watch over the spurious corpse. Suddenly Marko sat up. With his right hand he pulled out the nail from his left hand, grabbed hold of the widow by her red hair, and drove the nail into her neck. Then he pulled out the nail from his right hand with his left hand and drove it into her forehead. He then pulled out the stone thorn that pierced his feet and used it to stab her eyes. When the executioners returned, they found on the beach the convulsed corpse of an old woman instead of the body of a naked hero. The storm had waned, but the short-winded boats pursued in vain the swimmer who had vanished inside the belly of the waves. It seems unnecessary to add that Marko reached his own country and stole the beautiful girl who had awakened his smile, but it is neither his glory nor his happiness that moves me. What moves me is that exquisite euphemism, the smile on the tortured man's lips for whom desire is the sweetest torment. Look: evening is falling; one could almost imagine on the beach at Kotor the small group of executioners working to the glimmer of their burning coals, the dancing young girl, and the young man who could not resist beauty."

"A strange story," the archaeologist said. "But the version you have offered us is most certainly a recent one. There must be another, earlier one. I shall look it up."

"You would be wrong to do so," said the engineer. "I have passed it on to you exactly as it was told to me by the peasants in the village where I spent last winter, occupied with the drilling of a tunnel for the Orient Express. I do not wish to speak ill of your Greek heroes, Loukiadis: they would shut themselves up in a tent in a fit of savage anger; they would howl with grief over their dead friends' bodies; they would drag by their feet around conquered cities the corpses of their enemies, but, believe me, the *Iliad* is lacking such a smile from Achilles."

THE MILK OF
DEATH

The long, dappled line of tourists stretched along Ragusa's main street. Braided hats and opulent embroidered jackets swinging in the wind at the entrance of the shops tempted the eyes of travelers in search of inexpensive gifts or costumes for the masked balls held on board ship. It was as hot as only hell can be. The bald Herzegovinian mountains kept Ragusa under the fire of burning mirrors. Philip Mild entered a German alehouse where several fat flies were buzzing in the stifling gloom. Paradoxically, the restaurant's terrace opened onto the Adriatic, which sprang up suddenly in the very heart of the city, there where one would least expect it, and yet that sudden burst of blue did nothing but add yet another color to the motley of the Market Square. A sickening stench rose from a pile of fish leftovers picked clean by almost unbearably white seagulls. There was not a breath of sea air. Philip's friend, the engineer Jules Boutrin, sat at a small zinc table, holding a drink in the shade of a fire-colored parasol that from afar seemed like a large orange floating on the waters.

"Tell me another story, old friend," Philip said, dropping heavily into a chair. "I need both a whiskey and a story told beside the sea—the most beautiful and the least true of all stories imaginable—to make me forget the contradictory and patriotic lies in the papers I just bought on the quay. The Italians insult the Slavs, the Slavs the Greeks, the Germans insult the Russians, the French insult England almost as much as they insult Germany. I imagine they are all in the right. Let's change the subject . . . What were you doing yesterday in Scutari, where you insisted on seeing with your very own eyes God knows what engines?"

"Nothing," the engineer replied. "Apart from glancing at a few irrigation works, I spent most of my time in search of a tower. I had heard so many old Serbian women tell me the story of the Scutari Tower that I felt the need to see its crumbling bricks and to find out whether, as they say, a white trickle really flows from it. But time, wars, and peasants anxious to strengthen their farmhouse walls have demolished it, stone by stone, and the memory of the tower remains only in old wives' tales . . . By the way, Philip, are you lucky enough to have what is commonly known as a good mother?"

"I should hope so," the young Englishman replied with irony. "My mother is beautiful, slim, powdered and painted, hard as a shopwindow's reflecting glass. What more can I tell you? When we are out together, I am taken for her older brother."

"There: you are like the rest of us. To think of

the fools who argue that our times lack a sense of poetry, as if we had no surrealists, no prophets, no movie stars, no dictators. Believe me, Philip, what we lack is reality. Our silk is artificial, our horribly synthetic food resembles the make-believe dishes with which mummies are stuffed, and our women, who have become immune to unhappiness and old age, are, however, no longer alive. It is only in the legends of semi-barbaric countries that we still find these creatures rich in tears and milk, creatures whose children we would be proud to be. Where have I heard tell of a poet who was incapable of loving any woman because in another life he had met Antigone? A man after my own heart . . . A few dozen mothers and women in love, from Andromache to Griselda, have made me wary of these unbreakable dolls whom we take to be real.

"Let Isolde be my mistress, and let the lovely Aude, Roland's beloved, be my sister . . . But the one I would have chosen to be my mother is a very young girl from an Albanian legend, the wife of a chieftain from these regions . . .

"There were three brothers, and they were building a tower to serve as a lookout against Turkish robbers. They had undertaken the construction themselves, either because it was difficult or too expensive to hire laborers, or because, like true countryfolk, they trusted only their own hands, and their wives took turns bringing them lunch. But each time they managed to reach the point where they were able to place a bunch of herbs on the finished roof, the night wind and the mountain witches would topple their tower as God had once felled Babel. There are many reasons why a tower should not stand, and blame can be laid on the workers' lack of skill, on the unwillingness of the land, or on the insufficient strength of the cement binding the stones. But the Serbian, Albanian, and Bulgarian peasants will admit only one reason for such a disaster: they know that a building will crumble if one has not taken the precaution of walling into the base a man or a woman whose skeleton will support that weighty body of stone until Judgment Day. In Arta, in Greece, you are shown a bridge where a young girl was walled in: a wisp of her hair has sprung through a crack and droops over the water like a blond plant. The three brothers began to look at one another with suspicion, and were careful not to cast a shadow on the rising walls, because it is possible, for want of a better thing, to wall up into an unfinished tower that dark extension of a man which is perhaps his soul, and he whose shadow is so imprisoned dies as one suffering from a broken heart.

"Therefore, in the evening, each of the three brothers would sit as far as possible from the fire, fearing that one of them might approach silently from behind, throw a sack on the shadow, and carry it away, half choking, like a black pigeon. The eagerness which they had put into their work began to wane, and despair instead of weariness bathed their dark foreheads in sweat.

At last, one day, the eldest brother called the others to him and said: 'Little brothers, brothers with whom I share blood, milk, and baptism; if our tower remains unfinished, the Turks will once again slither up the banks of our lake, hiding behind the reeds. They will rape our farm girls; they will burn in our fields the promise of future bread; they will crucify our peasants on the scarecrows of our orchards, and our orchards will become a fattening ground for crows. Little brothers, we need each other, and a three-leaf clover should not sacrifice one of its three leaves. But each of us has a young, strong wife whose shoulders and fine neck are well accustomed to carrying loads. Let us not decide anything ourselves, my brothers: let us leave the choice to chance, God's figurehead. Tomorrow, at dawn, we shall wall into the foot of the tower whichever one of our wives brings us our food. I ask you but to be silent one night, oh, my brothers, and let us not embrace with too many tears and sighs the one who, after all, has two chances in three of still being alive at sunset.'

"It was easy for him to speak as he did, because he secretly hated his young wife and wanted to be rid of her, so as to replace her with a beautiful Greek girl with fiery hair. The second brother made no complaints, because he had made up his mind to warn his wife upon his return, and the only one to object was the youngest, because he usually kept his promises. Moved by the magnanimity of his brothers, who seemingly renounced what they held dearest in the world in favor of their common task, he ended up allowing himself to be convinced and promised to remain silent throughout the night.

"They returned from the fields at that hour of dusk in which the ghost of the dying light still haunts the countryside. The second brother reached his tent in a foul mood and ordered his wife to help him take off his boots. As she knelt in front of him, he threw his boots in her face and said: 'I've now been wearing this shirt for eight full days, and Sunday will come and I will not have a stitch of white linen to wear. Damn good-for-nothing, tomorrow at the break of day you shall go down to the lake with your basket of washing and you shall stay there till nightfall, with your brushes and your scrubbing board. If you move as much as a hair's breadth away, you shall die.'

"And the young woman promised, trembling, to spend the entire day washing.

"The eldest returned home fully resolved not to say anything to his wife, whose kisses irritated him and whose heavy beauty no longer pleased him. But he had one weakness: he talked in his sleep. That night, the buxom Albanian matron lay awake, wondering what could have displeased her lord and master. Suddenly she heard her husband mutter, as he pulled the blanket over himself: 'Dear heart, my own dear little heart, soon you'll be a widower . . . How peacefully we'll live, cut off from the dark-skinned hag, by the strong stones of the tower . . .'

"But the youngest brother entered his tent, pale and resigned to his fate like a man who has just met Death along the road, its scythe over its shoulder, on its way to reap its harvest. He kissed his child in its wicker cradle, tenderly took his young wife in his arms, and all night long she heard him sobbing against her heart. But the discreet young woman did not ask the cause of such great sadness, because she did not wish to force him to confide in her, and she had no need to know the nature of his sorrows in order to console him.

"The following morning, the three brothers took

their pickaxes and hammers and set off toward the tower. The second brother's wife prepared her basketful of linen and knelt down in front of the eldest brother's wife: 'Sister,' she said. 'Sister dear, it is my turn to take the men their food, but my husband has ordered me, under threat of death, to wash his white linen shirts, and my basket is now full.'

" 'Sister, sister dear,' said the wife of the eldest brother. 'Willingly would I go take our men their food, but last night a demon crept into one of my teeth . . . Ouch! ouch! All I can do is cry out in pain . . .' And she clapped her hands unceremoniously to summon the wife of the youngest brother.

" 'Wife of our youngest brother,' she said, 'dearest little wife of our youngest one, go in our place to feed the men, because the road is long, our feet are tired, and we are not as young or as nimble as you are. Go, little one, and we will fill your basket with delicious things to eat so that the men will greet you with a smile, as a messenger who will make their hunger vanish.'

"And the basket was filled with fish from the lake, preserved in honey and currants, rice wrapped in vine leaves, cheese made from ewe's milk, and salted-almond cakes. The young woman carefully gave her child into the arms of her sisters-in-law and set off along the road, alone, her load upon her head, her fate around her neck like a holy medallion, invisible to all eyes, on which God Himself might have written what death awaited her, and what place in His heaven.

"As soon as the three men glimpsed her from afar, the small figure still indistinct, they ran toward her, the two elder ones uneasy about the success of their plans, and the youngest praying to God. The eldest swallowed an oath as he saw that it was not his dark-skinned wife, and the second thanked the Lord out loud for having spared his washerwoman. But the youngest knelt down, clasped in his arms his young wife's thighs, and, sobbing, begged her forgiveness. Then he dragged himself to his brothers' feet and implored their pity. Finally he stood up, the blade of his knife glittering in the sun. A hammer's blow on his neck sent him gasping for air onto the side of the road. The frightened young woman let her basket fall, scattering the food, to the delight of the shepherd dogs.

"When she realized what was happening, she lifted her hands to heaven. 'Brothers whom I have never failed, brothers by the wedding ring and the priest's blessing, do not put me to death, but rather send word to my father, head of a mountain clan, and he will provide you with a thousand servants for you to sacrifice. Do not kill me: I am so fond of life. Do not place between my loved one and myself a wall of stone.'

"Suddenly she said no more, because she realized that her young husband, lying on the roadside, no longer blinked his eyes, and that his black hair was stained with brains and blood. She let herself be led, neither crying out nor weeping, to the niche cut out of the tower's round wall; seeing that she was going to die, she felt she could save her tears. But when the first brick was laid in front of her sandaled feet, she remembered her child who loved nibbling at her red shoes, like a playful puppy. Hot tears rolled down her cheeks and mingled with the cement that the trowel smoothed down on the stone.

" 'Little feet,' she moaned, 'never again will you carry me to the top of the hill to show my body a little sooner to the gaze of my best beloved. Never again will you feel the coolness of running water, until angels wash you on the morning of Resurrection.'

"The wall of bricks and stones rose to the height of her knees covered by a skirt of golden cloth. Erect within her niche, she looked like an image of Mary standing behind her altar.

" 'Farewell, dear knees,' said the young woman.

'Never again will you rock my child; never again will I fill my lap with delicious fruit, sitting beneath the lovely orchard tree that gives both nourishment and shade.'

"The wall grew a little higher, and the young woman continued: 'Farewell, dear little hands, hanging down both sides of my body, hands that shall no longer cook the dinner, hands that shall no longer twist the wool, hands that shall no longer lock yourselves around my best beloved. Farewell, my thighs, and you, my belly, you shall never again be great with child or love. Children whom I might have given birth to, little brothers whom I have not had time to give to my only son, you shall keep me company in this prison which shall also be my tomb, and where I shall stand, sleepless, until Judgment Day arrives.'

"The stone wall now reached her bosom, when suddenly a trembling shook the young woman's body and her imploring eyes shone with a look that was like the gesture of two outstretched hands. 'My brothers,' she said. 'Not for my sake, but for the sake of your dead brother, think of my child and do not let him starve. Do not wall up my bosom, my brothers, but allow him access to my breasts beneath the embroidered blouse, and bring my child to me every day, at dawn, at midday, and at dusk. As long as I have a few drops of life in me, they will flow down to the tips of my breasts to feed the child I brought into this world, and when the day comes when all my milk is gone, he shall drink my soul. Allow me this, evil brothers, and if you do, my beloved husband and I shall not cast blame on you when we meet again in God's house.'

"The frightened brothers agreed to grant this last wish and left a space of two bricks at the height of her breasts.

"Then the young woman murmured: 'Dear brothers, place your bricks in front of my mouth, because the kiss of the dead frightens the living, but allow an opening in front of my eyes so that I may see if my milk is doing my child good.'

"They did as she said, and a horizontal gap was left at the height of her eyes. At dusk, at the time when she used to feed her child, he was brought to her down the dusty road lined with low bushes that had been gnawed at by the goats, and the prisoner greeted the infant's arrival with cries of joy and blessings on the heads of the two brothers. Rivers of milk flowed from her hard, warm breasts, and when the child, made of the same stuff as her heart, fell asleep against her bosom, she sang with a voice muffled by the thickness of the brick wall. As soon as her child was plucked from her breast, she ordered he be taken to the campsite to sleep, but all night long the tender chant rose toward the stars, and the lullaby sung from a distance was enough to stop him from crying. The following morning she sang no more, and with a feeble voice she asked how Vania had spent the night. On the next day she fell silent, but she was still breathing, for her breasts, haunted by her respiration, rose and fell imperceptibly inside their cage. A few days later her breath followed her voice, and yet her now motionless breasts lost nothing of their sweet fountain-like abundance, so that the child asleep in the valley of her bosom could still hear her heart. And then the heart that had served her life so well slowed down its pace. Her languishing eyes died out like the reflection of stars in a waterless cistern, and nothing could be seen through the gap except two glassy eyeballs that no longer gazed upon the sky. These, in turn, changed to water and left in their place two empty sockets at the bottom of which Death could be perceived. But the young breasts remained intact and, for two whole years, the miraculous flow continued, until the child himself, weaned, turned his head from the milk.

"Only then did the exhausted breasts crumble to dust and on the brick sill nothing was left but a handful of white ashes. For several centuries, mothers moved by the tale came to trace with their finger the grooves made by the marvelous milk along the red brick; later the tower itself disappeared, and the heavy arches no longer weighed down on the light female skeleton. At last the brittle bones themselves were dispersed, and all that is left here is an old Frenchman roasted by this infernal heat, who tells this story to whoever comes along, a story as worthy of a poet's tears as that of Andromache."

Just then a gypsy woman, horribly covered in golden frippery, came up to the table where the two men were seated. In her arms she held a child, whose sickly eyes were half hidden by a bandage of rags. She bowed deeply, with the insolent servility common only to races of kings and beggars, and her yellow skirts swept the ground. The engineer pushed her away brusquely, deaf to her voice, which rose from a begging tone to a curse.

The Englishman called her back to give her a dinar. "What has come over you, you old dreamer?" he said with impatience. "Her breasts and necklaces are certainly worth those of your Albanian heroine. And the child she carries is blind."

"I know that woman," Jules Boutrin answered. "A doctor from Ragusa told me her story. For months she has been rubbing disgusting ointments on her child's eyes, ointments that swell his eyelids and make passersby pity him. He can still see, but soon he will be as she wishes him to be: blind. That woman will then be certain of her income for the rest of her life, because the care of an invalid is a profitable business. There are mothers . . . and then there are mothers."

THE LAST LOVE OF
PRINCE GENJI

When Genji the Resplendent, the greatest seducer ever to have astounded Asia, reached his fiftieth year, he realized that the time had come to begin his death. His second wife, Murasaki, Princess Wisteria, whom he had loved so deeply throughout so many conflicting infidelities, had preceded him into one of those paradises for the dead who have acquired some sort of merit during the course of this changing and difficult life, and Genji felt tormented by his inability to remember her smile, exactly as it was, or even that certain pout she would make before breaking into tears. His third wife, the Princess of the Western Palace, had been unfaithful to him with a young kinsman, just as he, in the days of his youth, had deceived his father with an adolescent empress. The same play began once more on the world's stage, but he knew that this time the role chosen for him would be that of an aging lover, in which case he preferred to play the role of ghost. For that reason, he distributed his worldly possessions, pensioned off his servants, and went off to end his days in a hermit's abode that he had ordered built upon the mountainside. One last time he crossed the city, followed only by two or three devoted friends who could not bear to say farewell to him, and thereby to their own youth. In spite of the early hour, the women were already pressing their faces against the slender lattices of the shutters. They whispered out loud that Genji was still very handsome, and this proved to the Prince once again that it was high time he left.

It took them three days to reach the retreat set in the midst of the wild countryside. The hut stood at the foot of a century-old maple tree; it was autumn, the leaves of the beautiful tree lined the brown straw roof with a golden thatch. Life in this lonely spot turned out to be simpler and harder than the long exile in foreign lands which Genji had undergone during his tempestuous youth, and this refined nobleman finally was able to let his soul fully enjoy the supreme luxury of possessing nothing. Soon the early cold weather announced itself; the mountainside was covered in snow like the ample folds of soft winter clothing, and mist snuffed out the sun. From dawn to dusk, by the thin light of a miserly brazier, Genji read the Scriptures and found in the austere verses a flavor that even the most moving love poems now lacked. But soon he realized that his sight was growing dim, as if all the tears he had shed over his fragile mistresses had burned out his eyes, and he was forced to realize that for him darkness would begin before death. From time to time, a frozen courier would arrive from the capital, tapping his feet swollen with weariness and frostbite, and would respectfully deliver the messages from Genji's family and friends who wished to visit him once more in this life, before the uncertain and endless meetings in other existences to come. But Genji was afraid of inspiring in his guests pity or respect, two feelings he abhorred and to which he much preferred oblivion. He would shake his head sadly, and this Prince famous for his talent both as poet and as calligrapher would send the messenger back with a blank sheet of paper. Little by little, the dealings with the capital became fewer; the wheel of seasonal holidays continued to turn far from the Prince who used to orchestrate them with a tap of his fan, and Genji, letting himself drift shamelessly into the sadness of solitude, made his eyesight increasingly worse because he no longer felt ashamed of crying.

Two or three of his old mistresses had offered to come and share his loneliness so full of memories. The tenderest letters were from the Lady-from-the-Village-of-Falling-Flowers, an ex-concubine of middle-class birth and mediocre beauty. She had faithfully served as lady-in-waiting to Genji's other wives, and for eighteen years she had loved the Prince without ever tiring of her suffering. From time to time she would visit him at nightfall, and these encounters, rare as stars on a rainy night, had sufficed to light up the poor life of the Lady-from-

the-Village-of-Falling-Flowers. With no illusions
about her beauty, or her intelligence, or her birth,
the Lady alone among so many of Genji's mistresses
felt gently grateful toward him, because she did not
believe it was natural for him to have loved her.

Seeing that her letters remained unanswered, she
hired a modest train of servants and had them
take her to the hut of the solitary Prince. Timidly
she pushed open the door of interwoven branches;
she knelt down with a humble little laugh, to apolo-
gize for being there. This happened at a time when
Genji could still recognize his visitors' faces, if they
came quite close. A bitter rage overtook him at the
sight of this woman who awakened in him the sharp-
est memories of days gone by, not so much because
of her own presence, but mainly because her sleeves
still bore the perfume used by his late wives. She
sadly begged him to keep her by his side, at least as
a handmaid. Merciless for the first time in his life,
Genji drove her away, but she had remained friends
with the handful of old men who waited on the
Prince, and from time to time they gave her news
of him. She, cruel for the first time in her life,
watched from a distance the progress of Genji's
blindness, as a woman impatient to meet her lover
waits for night to fall completely.

When she learned that he was almost totally
blind, she discarded her city robes and put on a

short coarse dress such as young peasant girls wear; she did up her hair in country-girl fashion, and she picked up a bundle of cloths and pottery, like those sold in village fairs. Dressed up in this manner, she asked to be taken where the voluntary exile lived, among wild deer and forest peacocks. The last stretch of the road she walked, so that the dirt and the weariness of the journey would help her play her part.

The tender spring rains fell from the heavens on the soft earth, drowning the last glimmers of dusk: it was the hour when Genji, wrapped in his strict monk's cloak, slowly made his way along the path from which his old servants had cleared even the smallest pebble, to prevent him from tripping. His vacant face, betraying no emotion, tarnished by blindness and the encroachments of old age, seemed like a leaden mirror whose beauty reflected only itself, and the Lady-from-the-Village-of-Falling-Flowers had no need to feign tears.

The sound of a woman sobbing startled Genji, and he slowly turned toward the source of the weeping. "Woman, who are you?" he asked uneasily.

"I am Ukifune, daughter of So-Hei, a farmer," said the Lady, not forgetting to put on a village accent. "I went into the city with my mother, to buy some material and a few pots, because I am to be married on the next moon. But I lost my way along the mountain paths, and I am crying because I am afraid of the wild boars, and the demons, and the lust of men, and the ghosts of the dead."

"You are soaking wet, my child," said the Prince, placing a hand on her shoulder.

She was indeed sodden, down to her very bones. The touch of that hand, so well known, made her tremble from the tip of her hair to the toe of her naked foot, but Genji thought that it was the cold that made her shiver.

"Come into my hut," the Prince continued in an enticing voice. "You can warm yourself by my fire, even though it contains more ashes than coals."

The Lady followed him, carefully imitating the clumsy walk of a peasant. Both crouched down by the almost dead fire. Genji stretched his hands toward the warmth, but the Lady hid her fingers, too delicate for a country girl.

"I am blind," sighed Genji after a moment. "You can, without any scruples, take off your wet clothes, my child, and warm your naked body by my fire."

Meekly the Lady took off her peasant's dress. The fire lent a blush to her slender body, which seemed carved in the palest amber.

Suddenly Genji murmured: "I have deceived you, my child, because I am not yet totally blind. I can make you out through a mist that is perhaps nothing but the halo of your own beauty. Let me put my hand on your still-trembling arm."

Thus the Lady-from-the-Village-of-Falling-Flowers became once again the mistress of the Prince, of Prince Genji, whom she had humbly loved for more than eighteen years. She did not forget to feign the tears and shyness of a young girl with her first love. Her body had remained surprisingly youthful, and the Prince's eyesight was too weak to make out her few gray hairs.

When their embraces ended, the Lady knelt before the Prince and said: "I have deceived you, Prince. I am indeed Ukifune, daughter of So-Hei, the farmer, but I did not lose my way in the mountain. Prince Genji's fame has reached the village, and I have come here of my own accord, in order to discover love in your arms."

Genji rose with difficulty, like a pine tree wavering under the blows of the wind and cold. He cried out in a wheezing voice: "Woe to you who have brought to my mind the image of my worst enemy, the beautiful Prince of fiery eyes whose image keeps me awake at night . . . Go!"

And the Lady-from-the-Village-of-Falling-Flowers left, regretting her mistake.

·

During the following weeks, Genji remained alone, in pain. He realized with disappointment that he was still caught in the snares of this world, and felt barely prepared for the relinquishing and the renewal expected in the next. The visit of farmer So-Hei's daughter had awakened in him an old taste for these creatures with slim wrists, long conical breasts, sad and docile laughter. Since blindness began to steal over him, his sense of touch had become his only means of reaching the beauty of the world, and the landscapes into which he had escaped to seek solace comforted him no longer, because the murmur of a stream is more monotonous than the voice of a woman, and the curves of hills and the wisps of clouds are made for those who can see, and hover too far away to allow us to caress them.

Two months later, the Lady-from-the-Village-of-Falling-Flowers tried once again. This time she dressed and perfumed herself carefully, but she deliberately arranged her garments to seem a little too tight-fitting and too coyly elegant, and her perfume to be discreet but commonplace, suggesting the lack of imagination of a young woman from an honorable province clan who had never been to court.

On this occasion, she engaged porters and an imposing chair, which lacked, however, the latest city improvements. She contrived to reach the environs of Genji's hut after nightfall. Summer had preceded her into the mountain. Genji, seated at the foot of the maple tree, was listening to the crickets sing.

She came close to him, half hiding her face behind a fan, and murmured in confusion: "I am Chūjo, wife of Sukazu, a nobleman of the seventh rank from the province of Yamato. I left on a pilgrimage to the Temple of Ise, but one of my porters has just hurt his foot, and I cannot continue on my way until dawn. Show me a hut where I might pass the night without fear of slander, and where my servants may rest."

"Where is a young woman better protected from slander than in the house of a blind old man?" said the Prince bitterly. "My hut is too small for your servants, who can settle down under this tree, but I will let you have the only mattress in my retreat."

He rose, feeling his way, to lead her. Not once did he lift his eyes toward her, and by this sign she realized that he was now fully blind. When she was lying on the mattress of dry leaves, Genji once again took up his melancholy post at the door of the hut. He felt sad; he did not even know whether the young woman was beautiful.

The night was warm and clear. The moon gave a pale hue to the uplifted face of the blind man, who seemed carved in white jade.

After a long moment, the Lady left her forest bedding and came to join him on the doorstep. She said with a sigh: "The night is lovely and I am not sleepy. Allow me to sing one of the songs of which my heart is full."

And without waiting for an answer, she sang a ballad the Prince loved well, having heard it often in times gone by from the lips of his favorite wife, Princess Wisteria. Genji, with a heavy heart, listlessly drew near the stranger. "Where are you from, young lady, you who know the songs that were loved in my youth? Harp on which old-fashioned tunes are played, let me lay a hand on your strings."

And he caressed her hair. After a moment, he asked: "Alas, is your husband not younger and more handsome than I am, young lady from Yamato?"

"My husband is less handsome and seems not as young as you" was the Lady-from-the-Village-of-Falling-Flowers's simple answer.

In this fashion, the Lady, in her new disguise, became the mistress of Prince Genji, to whom she had once belonged. In the morning she helped him prepare his hot gruel, and Prince Genji said to her: "You are skillful and tender, young lady, and I do not think that even Prince Genji, so fortunate in love, had a mistress gentler than you."

"I have never heard the name Prince Genji before," said the Lady, shaking her head.

"What?" cried out Genji bitterly. "Has he been so soon forgotten?"

And all day long he remained in a somber mood. The Lady understood that she had made a mistake for the second time, but Genji did not speak of sending her away and seemed happy to hear the rustle of her silk dress on the grass.

·

Autumn arrived, changing the mountain trees into spirits arrayed in purple and gold, fated to die with the first cold. The Lady would describe the grayish tans, the golden tans, the mauve tans to Genji, careful to mention them as if by chance, and each time she avoided helping him in too obvious a manner. She charmed Genji continuously by producing ingenious flower garlands, dishes refined because of their simplicity, new lyrics to old moving and poignant tunes. She had displayed these charms before, as the fifth concubine, in her pavilion, where Genji would visit her but where, distracted by other loves, he had failed to notice them.

Toward the close of autumn, fever rose from the marshes. Insects swarmed in the infected air and each intake of breath was like a gulp of water drunk at a poisoned spring. Genji became ill and lay on his bed of dead leaves, with the knowledge that he would never rise again. He felt ashamed, in front of the Lady, of his weakness and of the humiliating care to which his illness forced him, but this man who had always, throughout his life, searched in every experience for both the singular and the heart-rending could not help savoring what this new and miserable intimacy added to two beings tenderly bound by love.

One morning, while the Lady was massaging his legs, Genji propped himself up on his elbow and, feeling for the Lady's hands, murmured: "Young lady, you who are nursing a man about to die: I have deceived you. I am Prince Genji."

"When I first came to you, I was but an ignorant woman from the provinces," said the Lady, "and I knew not who Prince Genji was. Now I know that he was the most handsome and most desirable among men, but you have no need to be Prince Genji to be loved."

Genji thanked her with a smile. Since his eyes had grown silent, it seemed as if his sight fluttered upon his lips.

"I'm going to die," he said with difficulty. "I cannot complain of a destiny I share with the flowers, the insects, and the stars. In a universe where everything passes as in a dream, we would resent happiness that would last forever. I am not sorry to know that objects, beings, hearts are perishable, because part of their beauty lies in this very misfortune. What pains me is that they are unique. In the old days, the certainty of obtaining a singular revelation from each moment of my life was the brightest of my secret pleasures: now I will die ashamed, like the privileged spectator at a sublime feast that will not take place twice. Dear objects, your only witness is a dying blind man . . . Other women will blossom, as striking as those I once loved, but their smile shall be different, and the beauty spot that was my passion shall have moved along their amber cheek barely an atom's width. Other hearts will burst beneath the weight of an unbearable love, but their tears shall not be our tears. Hands moist with desire shall continue to join under the cherry trees in bloom, but the same rain of petals does not fall twice on the same human bliss. I feel like a man carried away by a flood, who wishes he might find a single corner of dry land to leave there a few yellowed letters and a few fans, the hues of which have faded . . . What will you become when I am no longer there to be moved by you, memory of the Blue Princess, my first wife, whose love I believed in only on the day after her death? And you, unhappy memory of the Lady-of-the-Convulvulus-Pavilion, who died in my arms because a jealous rival wished to be the only one to love me? And you, insidious memories of my far too beautiful mother-in-law and my far too youthful wife who taught me in turn how one suffers as either the accomplice or the victim of an infidelity? And you, subtle memory of the Lady-Cricket-in-the-Garden, who hid herself out of modesty, so that I was obliged to seek comfort in the arms of her younger brother, whose childish face reflected some of the lines of that timid woman's smile? And you, dear memory of the Lady-of-the-Long-Night, who was so tender to me, and who agreed to be but third in my household and in my heart? And you, poor little pastoral memory of farmer So-Hei's daughter, who loved in me only my past? And you, above all, you, delightful memory of tiny Chūjo, who now, this very instant, kneads my feet, and who will not have enough time to become a memory? Chūjo, whom I wish I had met earlier in my life, but it is also fair that a fruit be kept till late autumn . . ."

Distraught with sadness, he let his head fall on the hard pillow. The Lady-from-the-Village-of-Falling-Flowers leaned over him and whispered, trembling all over: "Was there not in your palace another woman, whose name you have not yet mentioned? Was she not tender? Was she not called Lady-from-the-Village-of-Falling-Flowers? Try to remember . . ."

But already Prince Genji had attained the peace which only the dead possess. The end of pain had erased all traces of satiety or bitterness from his face, and seemed to have made him believe that he was still a youth of eighteen. The Lady-from-the-Village-of-Falling-Flowers fell on the ground with an unrestrained cry; her salty tears ravaged her cheeks like a stormy rain, and her hair, torn out in tufts, drifted away like the fluff of silk. The only name that Genji had forgotten was precisely her own.

THE MAN WHO
LOVED THE NEREIDS

He stood on bare feet in the dust, heat, and stale smells of the port, beneath the narrow awning of a small café where several customers had let themselves fall on the chairs in the vain hope of protecting themselves from the sun. His old rust-colored trousers barely reached his ankles, and his pointed anklebones, the tips of his heels, his long, grazed, callused soles, his supple toes, all belonged to that race of intelligent feet, accustomed to the constant embrace of the air and the earth, hardened by the roughness of the stones, which in Mediterranean countries still allow a clothed man a little of the freedom of a man who is naked. These were agile feet, so different from the awkward, heavy ones trapped inside northern footwear . . . The faded blue of his shirt matched the tones of the sky bleached by the summer light; his shoulders and shoulder blades pierced through the tears in the cloth like lean rocks; his longish ears framed his head obliquely like the handles of a Greek vase; undoubtable traces of beauty could still be seen on his wan and vacant face, like the surfacing of an ancient broken statue in a wasteland. His eyes, like those of a sick animal, hid without distrust behind eyelashes as long as the eyelashes of mules; he held his right hand continuously stretched out, with the obstinate and insistent gesture of the archaic idols in the museums, who seem to demand from visitors the alms of their admiration; and an inarticulate braying issued from his wide-open mouth full of crooked teeth.

"Is he deaf and dumb?"

"He's certainly not deaf."

Jean Demetriadis, the owner of the large soap factory on the island, took advantage of a momentary distraction, during which the idiot's vague glance lost itself upon the sea, to let a drachma fall on the smooth stone slab. The light clink, half muffled by a fine coat of sand, was not lost on the beggar, who greedily picked up the small piece of white metal and then returned to his gazing and mournful position, much like a seagull perched on a quay.

"He's not deaf," Jean Demetriadis repeated, putting down in front of him his cup half full of unctuous black lees. "Both speech and reason were taken from him under such extraordinary conditions that sometimes I find myself envying him: I, a rich man, a reasonable man, who often finds nothing but boredom and emptiness along my path. This fellow Panegyotis, as he is called, was struck dumb at the age of eighteen for having seen the Nereids naked."

A shy smile appeared on Panegyotis's lips, hearing his name being mentioned. He did not seem to understand the meaning of the words spoken by this important man in whom he vaguely recognized someone who would protect him, but the tone, if not the words themselves, touched him. Happy in the knowledge that he was the subject of the conversation, and that perhaps there were more alms to be expected, he put forward his hand imperceptibly, with the wary movement of a dog brushing his master's knee with his paw, so as not to be forgotten at dinnertime.

"He is the son of one of the wealthiest peasants in my village," continued Jean Demetriadis, "and, an exception among my people, his parents are truly rich folk. They have more land than they know what to do with, a fine stone house, an orchard with several kinds of fruit trees, and vegetables in the garden; an alarm clock in the kitchen, a lamp lit on the icon wall—in a word, everything you could wish for. You could have said of Panegyotis what can rarely be said of a young Greek: that he had his fortune made for him. You could also say that he had the path of his future life laid out for him, a Greek path, dusty, stony, and monotonous, but here and there along the path, crickets sing, and you can stop at the door of taverns, which is pleasant enough. He used to help the old women beat the olives out of the trees; he oversaw the packing of the crates of grapes and the weighing of the bales of wool; in the discussions with the tobacco merchants, he discreetly stood up for his father, spitting in disgust at any proposal below the desired price; he was betrothed to the animal doctor's daughter, a good girl who once worked in my factory. As he was very handsome, folk saddled him with as many mistresses as there are women liking to be made love to in our country; it was rumored that he slept with the priest's wife; if the rumor was true, the priest did not hold it against him, because the priest did not care much for women in general, or for his own in particular, who, in any case, offers herself to anyone. Imagine Panegyotis's humble happiness: the love of beautiful women, the envy of men and sometimes their longing, a silver wristwatch, every two or three days a shirt, marvelously white, ironed by his mother, rice pilaf at midday and scented sea-green ouzo before supper. But happiness is brittle, and if men and circumstances don't destroy it, it is threatened by ghosts. Our ghosts are not like your northern spirits who come out only at night and live during the day in graveyards. Ours forgo the white sheets, and their skeletons are covered with flesh. But perhaps they are more dangerous than the spirits of the dead who at least have been baptized, have tasted life, have known what it is to suffer. These Nereids of our countryside are as innocent and as wicked as

Nature, which at times protects and at times destroys us. The ancient gods and goddesses are certainly dead, and the museums hold nothing but their marble corpses. Our nymphs are more like your fairies than like the image Praxiteles has led you to conceive. But our people believe in their powers; they exist as the earth exists, as the water and the dangerous sun. Summer light becomes flesh in them, and because of this the sight of them provokes vertigo and stupor. They come out only at the tragic hour of midday; they seem immersed in the mystery of high noon. If the peasants bar the doors of their houses before lying down for their afternoon nap, it is not against the sun, it is against them; these truly fatal fairies are beautiful, naked, refreshing and nefarious as water in which one drinks the germs of fever; those who have seen them languish sweetly with apathy and desire; those who have had the temerity to approach them are struck dumb for life, because the secrets of their love must never be revealed to common mortals. Now, one July morning, two of the sheep in Panegyotis's father's herd began to turn in circles. The epidemic spread quickly to the best animals, and the front yard of beaten earth soon became a bedlam of demented beasts. Panegyotis left all on his own, in the midday heat, under the midday sun, in search of the animal doctor, who lives on the far side of Mount Saint Elias, in a little village hidden along the seashore. At sunset, he had not returned. The concern of Panegyotis's father passed from his sheep to his son; the surrounding fields and the valleys were searched in vain; all night long, the women of the family prayed in the village chapel, which is simply a barn lit by two dozen candles, and where it seems as if at any minute Mary will come in to give birth to Jesus. On the following evening, after work, when the men usually sit in the village square in front of a tiny cup of coffee, a glass of water, or a spoonful of jam, a transfigured Panegyotis made his appearance, as changed as if he had walked through the Valley of Death. His eyes sparkled, but it seemed as if the whites and the pupils had devoured the irises; two months of malaria would not have given his skin a yellower hue; a slightly disgusting smile deformed his lips, from which no words poured forth.

"However, he had not yet become totally dumb. Broken syllables escaped from his mouth like the final gurgling of a dying fountain: 'The Nereids . . . Ladies . . . Nereids . . . Beautiful . . . Naked . . . Astounding . . . Blond . . . The hair, all blond . . .'

"These were the only words they managed to get out of him. Many times, during the following days,

he could be heard gently repeating to himself:
'Blond hair . . . Blond . . . ,' as if he were stroking
silk. That was all. His eyes stopped shining, but
his sight, which had acquired a fixed and vacant
look, now possesses singular properties: he can stare
at the sun without blinking; perhaps he finds pleasure in looking upon this dazzling blond object. I
was in the village during the first few weeks of his
delirium: no fever, no symptoms of sunstroke or
madness. In order to have him exorcised, his parents took him to a celebrated monastery not far
from here: he allowed himself to be handled with
the meekness of a sick lamb; but neither the cere-
monies of the Church nor the fumigations of in-
cense nor the magic rites performed by the old
wives in the village managed to expel from his blood
the mad sun-colored nymphs. The first days of his
newly acquired state passed in incessant comings
and goings: tirelessly, he returned to the spot where
the apparition had taken place. A spring flows there,
a spring where fishermen sometimes come to get
fresh water, a hollow valley, a field of fig trees from
which a path descends toward the sea. The people
of the village thought they had discovered light
traces of female feet on the thin grass and places
crushed by the weight of bodies. You can well
imagine the scene: the patches of sunlight in the

shadow of the fig trees, which is not really a shadow
but a greener, softer shade of light; the young man
warned by the female laughter and cries, like a
hunter by the sound of beating wings; the divine
young women lifting their white arms on which
blond hairs caught the sun; the shadow of a leaf
moving over a naked belly; a clear breast whose tip
is pink and not violet; Panegyotis's kisses devouring
those heads of blond hair, giving him the impression of filling his mouth with honey; his desire los-
ing itself between those blond legs. Just as there is
no love without a dazzling of the heart, there is no
true voluptuousness without the startling wonder
of beauty. Everything else is, at the most, a me-
chanical function, like hunger or thirst. To the
reckless young man the Nereids opened the gates
of a feminine world as different from that of the
island's girls as these are different from the ewes in
the herd; they made him drunk on the unknown,
they made him taste the exhaustion of a miracle,
they made him gaze on the evil sparks of happiness.
Some people say that he never stopped meeting
them, in the hot hours when these lovely midday
she-devils roam the countryside in search of love.
He seems to have forgotten even the face of his betrothed, from whom he turns away as if she were
a disgusting ape; he spits on the path of the priest's
wife, who was in tears for a good two months be-

fore consoling herself. The Nymphs stripped him
of his senses in order to better entangle him in their
games, like a sort of innocent faun. He no longer
works; he no longer cares about the passing of
months or days; he has become a beggar, and simply eats when he is hungry. He wanders about the
island, avoiding as far as possible the major roads;
he crosses fields and pine forests between bare hills;
and some say that a jasmine blossom placed on a dry
stone wall, a white pebble at the foot of a cypress,
are messages which tell him the time and place of
his next meeting with the fairies. The peasants say
that he will not grow old: like all those on whom
an evil spell has been cast, he will whither without
our ever knowing whether he is eighteen or forty
years old. But his knees tremble and shake, his soul
has left him never to return, and words will not
come to his lips ever again. Homer knew that those
who sleep with the golden goddesses have their
intelligence and their strength drained from them.
And yet I envy Panegyotis. He has left the world
of facts to enter that of illusions, and sometimes I
think that an illusion is perhaps the shape that the
innermost secret realities take in the mind's eye
of common folk."

"But look here, Jean," his wife said irritably.
"You don't really believe that Panegyotis actually
saw the Nereids?"

Jean Demetriadis did not answer, too busy half
lifting himself out of his chair to return the haughty
greeting of three passing foreigners. Three young
American girls in their comfortable white linen
clothes were walking listlessly across the sun-
drenched quay, followed by an old porter bent over
with the weight of provisions bought at the market; they held hands, like three girls on their way
home from school. One of them walked bareheaded,
myrtle sprigs stuck in her red hair, but the second
one wore an immense Mexican straw hat, and the
third a peasant woman's cotton scarf; dark sun-
glasses protected her eyes like a mask. The three
girls had settled on the island and had bought a
house far from the main roads: at night they fished
with a trident in their very own boat, and in autumn they hunted for quail; they socialized with
no one and looked after themselves, fearful of letting a housekeeper enter their tightly knit everyday
life; they isolated themselves to avoid gossip, pre-
ferring perhaps the slander. In vain I tried to inter-
cept the look Panegyotis cast upon these three
goddesses, but his distracted eyes remained empty
and lifeless: obviously, he failed to recognize his
Nereids dressed up as women. Suddenly he bent
over, with animal grace, to pick up yet another
drachma that had fallen out of one of our pockets,
and I saw, caught in the rough grain of his pea

jacket, which he carried hanging over one shoulder, clipped onto his suspenders, the only thing that could lend an imponderable proof to my conviction: the silky, slender, the lost thread of a single blond hair.

OUR-LADY-OF-
THE-SWALLOWS

Therapion the monk had been, in his youth, the most faithful disciple of the great Athanasius; he was graceless, austere, gentle only toward those creatures in whom he did not suspect the presence of demons. In Egypt, he had resurrected and evangelized mummies; in Byzantium, he had heard the confessions of emperors; he had come to Greece on the strength of a dream, fully intent on exorcising this land still under the influence of Pan's charms. He burned with rage at the sight of the sacred trees from which peasants suffering from fever hung rags supposed to shiver in their place with the slightest evening breeze, at the sight of the phalluses erected in the fields to force the earth to produce harvests, and at the sight of the clay gods tucked into crevices in the walls and fountainheads. With his own hands he had built a cramped hut on the banks of the Cephissus, careful to use only materials that had first been blessed. The peasants shared with him their meager food, but in spite of their being wan and pale, of their having been disheartened by famines and by wars that had befallen them, Therapion had never managed to turn their souls heavenward. They adored Jesus, Mary's son, arrayed in gold like the rising sun, but their obstinate hearts remained faithful to the deities who dwelt in trees or rose from the foaming waters; in the evening, they would place beneath the plane tree consecrated to the Nymphs a saucer of milk from the only goat they still had left; the boys would hide at midday among the clumps of trees to spy upon these onyx-eyed women who fed on thyme and honey. They were everywhere, daughters of the hard, dry land where that which elsewhere becomes mist at once takes on the shape and substance of reality. Their footsteps could be seen in the muddy beds of springs, and from afar the whiteness of their bodies mingled with their reflections on the rocks. Sometimes a mutilated Nymph would survive in the badly planed beam holding up a roof, and at night she could be heard moaning or singing. Almost every day, a sheep or a goat on which a spell had been cast would get lost in the mountains, and then, months later, only a small pile of bones would be found. The Evil Ones would lead children by the hand to dance on the edge of cliffs; their light feet would not touch the ground, but the abyss would devour their heavy little bodies. On other occasions, a young man, hot on their trail, would come down the mountain breathless, shivering with fever, having drunk death at a spring. After each disaster, Therapion the monk would make a fist at the woods where the Damned Ones hid, but the village people continued to care for these young, almost invisible fairies, and would forgive their mischief as one forgives the sun which unhinges madmen's brains, the moon which suckles the milk of sleeping mothers, and love which causes so much suffering.

The monk feared them like a pack of she-wolves, and they troubled him like a drove of harlots. These whimsical beauties never left him in peace: at night, he would feel their hot breath on his face, like that of an almost tame animal timidly roaming a room. If he ventured across the fields with the Last Sacraments for a sick person, he would hear at his heels their fitful, broken steps like those of young goats; if, in spite of his efforts, he happened to fall asleep at prayertime, they would playfully come to pull his beard. They did not try to seduce him, because they thought him ugly, comical, and too old in his thick robes of brown baize, and in spite of their own beauty they failed to arouse in him unclean longings, because their nakedness revolted him like the smooth flesh of the caterpillar or the slithery skin of the grass snake. However, they led him into temptation, because he would eventually doubt the wisdom of God who had fashioned so many worthless and dangerous creatures, as if Creation itself were nothing but an evil game in which

He had cared to indulge. One morning, the villagers found their monk busy cutting down the Nymphs' plane tree, and they felt doubly sorry, on the one hand because they feared the vengeance of the fairies, who might abandon them, taking with them the clear water springs, and on the other hand because the plane tree sheltered the spot where they used to meet and dance. But they did not complain to the holy man, for fear of falling out with Our Father who is in heaven, and who bestows both sun and rain. They held their tongues, and Therapion's scheming against the Nymphs was encouraged by this silence.

He never left the hut except with a couple of flints hidden in a fold of his sleeve, and in the evening, surreptitiously, when he was certain he could see no peasants in the deserted fields, he would set fire to an old olive tree whose cavernous trunk seemed to him to hide a goddess, or a young scaly pine tree whose resin wept tears of gold. A naked form would escape from among the leaves and run off to join its companions, motionless in the distance like frightened does, and the holy monk rejoiced at having destroyed one of the dens of Evil. Everywhere he set a Cross, and the young immortal creatures would stand back, fleeing the shadow of this splendid gibbet, leaving around the sanctified

village an increasingly vaster area of silence and solitude. But he kept up the struggle, step by step,
on the lowest slopes of the mountain, which de-
fended itself with spiny brambles and stone ava-
lanches, and from which it is much more difficult
to chase away the gods. Finally, surrounded by prayers and by flames, starved by the absence of offer-
ings, deprived of love since the young men from
the village had begun to stay away from them, the
Nymphs sought refuge in a deserted valley, where
a few black pine trees planted in the clay resembled
large birds lifting the red earth in their strong claws
and moving in the sky the thousand slender tips of
their eagle feathers. The streams that sprang here
beneath a few heaps of shapeless stones were too
cold to attract washerwomen or shepherd girls. A
cave gaped halfway up a hill, and it could be entered
only by an opening barely large enough to allow a
single body to pass. Since time immemorial, the
Nymphs had sought refuge there on nights on
which storms disrupted their play, because, like all
forest creatures, they feared the thunder; it was
also there that they slept on moonless nights. Young
shepherds boasted of having secretly entered the
cave, risking both the salvation of their souls and
their youthful strength, and they would not keep
quiet about the soft bodies half seen in the cool

darkness, and about the long hair guessed at rather than felt. For Therapion the monk, this cave, concealed in this side of the cliff, was like a cancer deep inside his own body, and standing at the mouth of the valley, his arms stretched toward the sky, immobile for hours on end, he begged heaven to help him destroy these dangerous remains of the race of gods.

Shortly after Easter, the monk called together the more faithful or more rustic among his congregation; he gave them pickaxes and lanterns, armed himself with a crucifix, and guided them through the maze of hills, in the soft spring darkness full of sap, anxious to make the most of that murky night. Therapion the monk stopped at the mouth of the cave and forbade his followers to enter, lest they be tempted. In the dull shadows he could hear the running streams, and the echo of a faint sound, soft as the breeze in the pine groves: the breathing of the Nymphs asleep dreaming of the childhood of the world, of a time when man had not yet come into being, and when the earth gave birth only to trees, animals, and gods. The peasants built a large fire, but they could not burn the cliff; the monk ordered them to prepare plaster and carry stones. In the first light of dawn, they had begun the construction of a small chapel set against the hillside, in front of the doomed cave. The walls were not yet dry, the roof was not yet laid on, the door was missing, but Therapion the monk knew that the Nymphs would not try to escape across that holy place which he had already consecrated and blessed. To be doubly sure, he had planted, deep inside the chapel, by the entrance to the cave, a large Christ painted on a cross with four arms of equal length, and the Nymphs, who can understand only smiles, retreated in horror at the sight of Our Crucified Lord's image. The first rays of the sun stretched timidly toward the cave's entrance: it was the hour when the unfortunate creatures usually emerged for their first meal of dew on the leaves of the neighboring trees; the prisoners sobbed, begging the monk to come and rescue them, and, in their innocence, they promised him their love if he helped them escape. All day long, the work continued, and well into the evening, tears could be seen falling from the stones, and one could hear coughs and hoarse moans like the cries of wounded beasts. On the following day, the roof was put in place and crowned with a bunch of flowers; the door was hung, and a large iron key was turned in the lock. That night the tired peasants returned to the village, but Therapion the monk lay down near the chapel he had built, and all night long the moaning of the prisoners kept him delightfully awake. And yet he felt for them, as he felt for a worm on which his feet might have trodden, or for the stem of a flower broken by the touch of his robes, but he was like a man rejoicing for having walled in between two bricks a nest of young vipers.

On the following day, the peasants brought along whitewash and splashed it on the inside and the outside of the chapel, which seemed to turn into a white dove pressed against the heart of the cliff. Two villagers, less frightened than the others, ventured inside the cave to paint its damp and porous walls, so that the water of the springs and the honey of the bees sustaining the waning life of the fairy maidens would stop flowing within the beautiful lair. The weakened Nymphs no longer had the strength to appear before humans; barely, here and there, a young tight mouth, two frail begging hands, the pale rose of a breast could be vaguely made out in the gloom. Or, from time to time, passing their large fingers stained with whitewash along the gnarled surface of the rocks, the peasants would feel a head of hair escape into the dark, lithe and trembling like those lichens that sometimes grow in abandoned and humid places. The broken bodies of the Nymphs would decompose into mist, or begin to crumble into dust like the wings of a dead butterfly; they still would moan, but one had to listen carefully to hear their feeble whining; only the souls of the Nymphs remained to cry.

All through the following night, Therapion the monk continued his prayer vigil at the entrance of the chapel, like an anchorite in the desert. He felt happy at the thought that before the new moon, the cries would have ceased, and the Nymphs, dead of starvation, would be but an unclean memory. He prayed to hasten the moment in which death would deliver his prisoners, because, in spite of himself, he had begun to pity them, and he was angry at himself for such shameful weakness. No one came to see him anymore; the village seemed to him as distant as if he lived on the far side of the world; on the other slope of the valley he could see nothing but red earth, pine trees, and a path almost hidden beneath the golden needles. He could hear nothing but those ever-diminishing cries, and the sound, hoarser and hoarser, of his own prayers.

That evening, he saw on the path a woman coming toward him. She was walking with her head bent, almost hunched over; her scarf and her cloak were black, but a strange radiance shone through the dark cloth, as if she had spread the cloak of night over the morning. In spite of her extreme youth, she had the gravity, the slow pace, the dignity of a very old woman, and her sweetness was that of mellow grapes or a scented blossom. Passing in front of the chapel, she stared closely at the monk, distracting him from his prayers.

"This path leads nowhere, woman," he said. "Where do you come from?"

"From the east, like the morning," she answered. "And what are you doing here, old monk?"

"I walled into this cave the Nymphs that still infested this region," said the monk, "and in front of the mouth of the site I built a chapel, which they dare not cross to escape, because they are naked, and, in their own fashion, they fear God. I am waiting for them to die of hunger and cold in their cave, and when that happens, God's peace will reign in the fields."

"And who told you that God's peace does not reach the Nymphs, as it reaches the deer and the herds of goats?" asked the young woman. "Do you not know that, at the time of Creation, God forgot to give wings to certain angels, who fell to earth and settled in the woods, where they became the forebears of the Nymphs and of Pan? And that others settled on a mountain, where they became the gods of Olympus? Do not, like the pagans, exalt the Creation at the expense of the Creator, but do not be scandalized either by His handicraft. And thank

God, from the bottom of your heart, for having created Diana and Apollo."

"My spirit cannot rise that high," said the old monk humbly. "The Nymphs disturb my congregation and endanger their salvation, for which I am responsible to God Himself, and that is why I shall chase them, if necessary, beyond the very gates of hell."

"And your zeal will be taken into account, honest monk," the young woman said, smiling. "But can you not see a way of reconciling the Nymphs' lives and your flock's salvation?"

Her voice was as sweet as the music of flutes. Uneasily, the monk bowed his head. The young woman put a hand on his shoulder and said gravely: "Monk, allow me to enter the cave. I am fond of caves, and I am moved by those who seek refuge in them. In a cave I gave birth to my child, and in a cave I entrusted him, without fear, into the hands of death, to suffer the second birth of Resurrection."

The hermit stepped aside to let her pass. Without hesitating, she walked to the mouth of the cave, hidden behind the altar. The large cross blocked the entrance; she gently moved it aside, like a familiar object, and stepped into the void.

Sharper wails were heard in the darkness, twitterings and a sound like the rustling of wings. The young woman spoke to the Nymphs in an unknown tongue, perhaps that of angels and birds. After a moment, she reappeared by the side of the monk, who had not ceased praying.

"Behold," she said, "and listen."

Innumerable small piercing cries came from inside her cloak. She opened it, and Therapion the monk saw that in the folds of her dress she bore hundreds of young swallows. She stretched out her arms, like a woman praying, and let the birds fly away. And then she said, in a voice as clear as the sound of a harp: "Go, my children."

The freed swallows soared into the evening sky, drawing with their beaks and their wings inscrutable signs. The old man and the young woman followed them for a moment with their eyes.

Then the traveler said to the hermit: "They will come back every year, and you will give them sanctuary in my church. Farewell, Therapion."

And Mary left, down the path that led nowhere, like a woman who cares little if the roads end because she knows the way to walk up to heaven. Therapion the monk went down to the village, and on the following day, when he climbed back to celebrate Mass, the cave of the Nymphs was lined with swallows' nests. They flew back and forth in the church, busily feeding their young, or strengthening their houses of clay, and Therapion the monk would frequently interrupt his prayers to follow tenderly their lovemaking games, because that which is forbidden to the Nymphs is allowed to the swallows.

APHRODISSIA,
THE WIDOW

They called him Kostis the Red because of his red hair, because he had laden his conscience with a fair quantity of spilled blood, and above all because he wore a red jacket when, full of insolence, he would come down to the horse fair and force a terrified peasant to either sell him his best mount at a low price or risk one of a number of sudden deaths. He had lived rooted in the mountain, a few hours' walk from the village of his birth, and his evil deeds had, for a long time, limited themselves to various political assassinations and the kidnapping of about a dozen lean sheep. He could have returned to his smithy untroubled, but he was one of those men who prefer, above everything else, the taste of fresh air and stolen food. Then two or three common-law murders had put the villagers on the warpath; they had hounded him as if he had been a wolf, and forced him out as if he had been a wild boar. Finally they had managed to capture him during the night of Saint George, and he had been brought back to the village thrown across a saddle, his throat slit like a beast's in a slaughterhouse; the three or four young men he had dragged along on his life of adventure had ended like him, riddled with bullets and carved by the blade. Their heads, planted on pitchforks, decorated the plaza atop the village; the bodies lay one on top of the other at the entrance to the cemetery; the victorious peasants celebrated the event, protected from the sun and the flies by their closed shutters, and the widow of the old Greek priest whom Kostaki had murdered six years earlier, on a deserted road, wept in her kitchen while washing out the goblets which she had offered, full of ouzo, to the peasants who had avenged her.

Aphrodissia the widow wiped her eyes and sat down on the kitchen's only bench, leaning both her hands on the edge of the table, and on her hands her chin, which trembled like that of an old woman. It was Wednesday, and she had not eaten since Sunday. It was also three days since she had last slept. Her muffled sobs shook her breast underneath the thick folds of her black worsted dress. She almost fell asleep in spite of herself, rocked by her own wailing; with a start, she sat up straight: the time of sleeping and forgetting had not yet come for her. For three days and three nights, the women from the village had waited in the square, whimpering every time a shot was carried through the mountain by a storm of echoes; and Aphrodissia's cries had grown louder than those of her companions, as would be expected from the widow of a character as respectable as the old priest lying for six years now in his tomb. She had felt sick when the peasants returned on the dawn of the third day

with their bloody load on a tired mule, and her
neighbors had been forced to carry her back into
the house where she had lived, away from everything, since her widowhood; however, as soon as
she was back home, she insisted upon offering the
avengers a drink. Hands and knees still trembling,
she had approached, one by one, each of the men
who spread through the room an almost unbearable odor of leather and fatigue, and as she was not
able to sprinkle with poison the slices of bread and
cheese she had cut for them, she had to satisfy herself by spitting on them secretly, and wishing the
autumn moon would soon rise above their graves.

It was then that she ought to have confessed her
entire life to them, bedevil their foolish minds or
justify their worst suspicions, pull deep over their
ears the truth which she had found both so easy
and so hard to hide from them over the past ten
years: her love for Kostis, their first meeting on a
secluded road, under a mulberry tree where she had
sought refuge during a hailstorm, and their passion
born with the suddenness of lightning on that
stormy night; her return to the village, her soul full
of anguish due more to fear than to repentance; the
intolerable week during which she had tried to part
with that man who had become for her dearer than
bread or water; and her second visit to Kostis on
the pretext of taking flour to the priest's mother,

who managed on her own a farm in the mountains; and the yellow skirt she wore in those days, which they had spread over themselves like a blanket, and it had seemed to them as if they were lying underneath a sheet of sun; and the night on which they had been forced to hide in the stable of an abandoned Turkish inn; and the young chestnut branches which brushed them refreshingly as they passed; and Kostis's arched back in front of her along paths where the slightest sudden movement risked startling a snake; and the scar she had not noticed on the first day, slithering down his neck; and the lustful, crazed looks he cast on her as on some precious stolen object; and his solid body of a man accustomed to living in the wild; and his reassuring laugh; and the way he had of mumbling her name when they made love.

She rose and waved her hand with a wide gesture toward the white wall on which two or three flies were buzzing. The fat flies that fed on filth were nothing but vermin, somewhat troublesome, which one allowed to come and go, softly and lightly, on one's skin; they had perhaps landed on that naked body, on that bleeding head; they had added their insult to the kicking of the children and the curious stares of the women. Oh, if only she could, with a quick swipe, do away with the entire village, the old women with poisonous tongues like wasps' stings;

and the young priest, drunk on the wine of Mass, who thundered in church against his predecessor's murder; and those peasants savaging Kostis's body like hornets on a honey-dripping fruit. Little did they imagine that Aphrodissia's mourning could have an object other than the old priest buried for the past six years in the most honorable corner of the cemetery: she had not been able to shout out to them that she cared for the life of that pompous drunkard as much as for the wooden seat of the privy at the far end of her garden.

And in spite of this, in spite of the snores that used to keep her awake and his unbearable habit of clearing his throat, she almost missed him, this credulous and vain old man who had allowed himself to be deceived, then terrorized, with the comic exaggeration of one of those jealous husbands who make one laugh on the screen of moving shadows: he had added an element of farce to the drama of their love. And it had been fun to wring the necks of the priest's chickens which Kostis carried away under his jacket, on the evenings when he crept secretly into the presbytery, and then blame the foxes for the theft. It had even been fun, one night when the old man had woken up because of the racket of their lovemaking beneath the plane tree, to spy at the window, carefully observing each of their movements in their shadows cast on the garden wall, grotesquely torn between the fear of scandal, the fear of a gunshot, and the wish for revenge. Aphrodissia blamed Kostis for only one thing: the murder of the old man who had served them, in spite of himself, as a blanket to hide their love.

Since her widowhood, no one suspected the dangerous meetings with Kostis on moonless nights, so that the dish of their happiness lacked the spice of a witness. When the suspicious eyes of the matrons had settled on the young woman's growing waist, all they imagined was that the priest's widow had allowed herself to be seduced by a traveling salesman, or by a farmhand, as if these were the kind of people with whom Aphrodissia would have deigned to go to bed. And she was forced to accept these suspicions gladly, swallowing her pride even more carefully than her revulsion. And when they saw her again a few weeks later, belly flat underneath the large skirts, they all wondered what Aphrodissia had done to get rid of her load so easily.

No one had imagined that the visit to the shrine of Saint Lukas had been an excuse, and that Aphrodissia had stopped barely a few miles from the village, at the hut of the priest's mother, who now agreed to bake Kostis's bread and patch his jacket. It was not because the old one had a tender heart, but because Kostis provided her with liquor and also because, in her youth, she as well had enjoyed love. And it was there that the child was born, and there that it had been necessary to stifle him between two mattresses, weak and naked like a newborn kitten, without even having bothered to wash him after the birth.

Finally, there had been the killing of the mayor by Kostis's companions, after which her beloved's bony hands began gripping the old hunting rifle tighter and tighter; and then those three days and three nights during which the sun had seemed to rise and set in blood. And tonight all would end in a joyful bonfire for which the tins of gasoline had already been piled up at the entrance to the cemetery; Kostis and his friends would be treated like those carcasses of mules one soaks in petrol so as not to have to bother burying them, and Aphrodissia had barely a few hours left, of high noon and solitude, to savor her mourning.

She lifted the latch and walked out onto the narrow strip of high ground that separated her from the cemetery. The piled-up bodies lay against the wall of dry stones, but Kostis was not difficult to recognize; he was the tallest, and she had loved him. A greedy peasant had taken his jacket to wear on Sundays; he lay almost naked. Two or three dogs licked the black trails of blood on the ground, and then, panting, returned to lie in a thin ribbon of shade. In the evening, at the hour in which the sun begins to grow harmless, small groups of women would start to assemble on the narrow terrace, examining the mole Kostis had between his shoulders. The men would kick the corpse over, to better soak in petrol the few bits of clothing that had been left on him; they would twist off the lids of the gasoline cans, rejoicing like grape gatherers opening a barrel. Aphrodissia touched the torn sleeve of the shirt she had sewn with her own hands as an Easter present for Kostis, and suddenly recognized her own name carved by him in the crook of his left arm. If eyes other than her own happened to fall upon those letters clumsily tattooed on the skin, the truth would certainly light up their spirits like the flames that would soon begin to dance upon the graveyard wall. She saw herself being stoned, buried beneath rocks. She could not, of course, tear off that arm which accused her with so much tenderness, or heat irons to obliterate those marks that were her undoing. She could never bring herself to wound again that body which had already bled so much.

The crowns of white metal that cumbered Stefan the priest's tomb sparkled from the other side of the low wall guarding the consecrated ground, and the unsightly mound of earth suddenly reminded her of the old man's fat belly. After being widowed, she had been left in that hovel barely a stone's throw from the cemetery: she had not complained about living in that isolated place where nothing but gravestones grew, because sometimes Kostis had been able to venture in the dead of night along that road which no other living creature took, and the gravedigger who lived in the house next to her own was as deaf as a corpse. Stefan the priest's tomb was separated from her hut by nothing except the graveyard wall, and it had seemed to them as if they went on with their caresses in the old man's very beard. Today that same solitude would allow Aphrodissia to carry out a plan worthy of her life of stratagems and recklessness, and pushing open the wooden gate cracked by the sun, she grabbed hold of the gravedigger's pickaxe and spade.

The earth was dry and hard, and Aphrodissia's sweat fell heavier than her tears. From time to time, the spade clanked against a stone, but in that deserted place the sound troubled no one; the whole village slept deeply after their meal. At last she heard, against the pickaxe, the dry sound of old wood, and the priest's casket, more brittle than the wood of a guitar, split under the blow, revealing bits of bone and shabby chasuble that were all that was left of the old man. With this debris, Aphrodissia made a pile, which she carefully pushed to one corner of the coffin, and then dragged Kostis's body to the pit, clutching it under the arms. Her old lover was a head taller than her husband, but the coffin was large enough for Kostis with his head cut off. Aphrodissia closed the lid, piled earth back on the tomb, covered the freshly dug mound with wreaths bought in Athens at the parish's expense, and smoothed out the dust on the path along which she had dragged her dead one. A body was now missing from the pile at the entrance to the graveyard, but the peasants were not going to search among the tombs to find it.

She sat down out of breath, and almost immediately stood up again, because she had begun to enjoy her gravedigger's task. Kostis's head was still up there, exposed to all indignities, speared on a pitchfork in the very spot where the village gave way to the rocks and the sky. Nothing was finished until she had completed her funeral rites, and she had to press on to take advantage of the hot hours during which the villagers, barricaded in their houses, slept, counted their drachmas, made love, and left the outside world to the sun.

Skirting the houses, she took the least frequented path to climb to the top of the village. Thin dogs slumbered in the narrow shade of the doorways; Aphrodissia kicked them as she passed, venting on them the rage she could not vent on their masters. Then, as one of the animals stood up, raising its hackles and letting out a long whine, she stopped for a moment to pacify it with wooings and pats. The air burned like a red-hot iron, and Aphrodissia drew her scarf over her forehead, because it would not do to collapse with sunstroke before finishing her task.

The path led onto a round white plaza. Higher up, there was nothing but large cliffs riddled with caves into which only desperadoes such as Kostis ventured, and from which strangers would be called back by the rough voices of the peasants if they as much as made a gesture to enter them. Higher still were only the eagles, and the sky, whose roads only the eagles know. The five heads of Kostis and his companions made, high on their pitchforks, the different bitter grimaces that only the dead can make. Kostis pursed his lips as if meditating on a problem which he had not had time to solve during his lifetime, such as the purchase of a horse or the ransom of some new captive, and, alone among his friends, he was not much changed by death, because he had always been naturally pale. Aphrodissia grabbed the head, lifting it from the pitchfork with the sound of torn silk; flies already stuck to the tears of blood on the eyelids. She was planning to hide it in her house, beneath the kitchen floor, or perhaps in a cave which only she knew, and she caressed the head, assuring it that they were safe.

She sat down in farmer Basil's field, under the

plane tree which curved its branches toward the square below. Beneath her feet, the cliffs rolled swiftly onto the plain, and the woods covering the land seemed from afar tiny patches of moss. In the far distance, the sea could be glimpsed between two mountain ridges, and Aphrodissia told herself that, had she been able to convince Kostis to escape upon those waves, she would not have to cradle now on her lap a head streaked with blood. Her grief, held back since the beginning of her misfortune, burst at last in vehement sobs like those of professional mourners, and, her elbows on her knees, her hands on her damp cheeks, she let her tears flow on the dead man's face.

"Hey, thief, you, the priest's widow—what are you doing in my orchard?"

Old Basil, armed with a billhook and a stick, leaned down from high above the road, and his suspicious anger made him look all the more like a scarecrow.

Aphrodissia jumped to her feet, covering Kostis's head with her apron. "I have only stolen a little of your shade, Uncle Basil, a little shade to cool my brow."

"What are you hiding in your apron, you thieving good-for-nothing widow? A pumpkin? A watermelon?"

"I am poor, Uncle Basil, all I have taken is a red, red watermelon. A red watermelon with black seeds."

"Show it to me, you liar, you black mole, and give me back what you have stolen."

Old Basil began to climb down the slope, brandishing his stick. Aphrodissia started to run toward the precipice, holding the corners of her apron in her hands. The slope became steeper and steeper, the road more and more slippery, as if the blood of the setting sun had spilled onto the stones. By now, Basil had stopped in his tracks and was yelling to the runaway to turn back; the road had become a path, and the path a trail of rocks. Aphrodissia could hear him, but in his words, torn by the wind, she made out only the need to escape from the village, from the lies, from the weight of hypocrisy, from the long punishment of becoming one day an old woman who is no longer loved. At last, a stone gave way under her foot, fell to the bottom of the precipice as if to show the way, and Aphrodissia the widow plunged into the abyss and the evening, taking with her the head all smeared with blood.

KALI BEHEADED

Kali, the terrible goddess, roams the Indian plains.

She can be seen both in the north and in the south, and at the same time in holy places and in the market squares. Women shudder as she passes; the young men, nostrils quivering, come out onto the thresholds, and even the little crying children know her name. Black Kali is beautiful and horrible. Her waist is so slender that the poets who sing about her compare her to the banana tree. Her shoulders are round like the rising autumn moon; her breasts are like buds about to burst; her hips sway like the trunk of the newly born elephant calf; and her dancing feet are like green shoots. Her mouth is as warm as life; her eyes as deep as death. In turn she gazes at herself in the bronze of night, in the silver of dawn, in the copper of dusk; in the gold of midday she stares at herself. But her lips have never smiled; a necklace of bones coils around her slender neck, and upon her face, paler than the rest of her body, her large eyes are pure and sad. Kali's face, eternally bathed in tears, is ashen and covered with dew like the uneasy face of dawn.

Kali is abject. She has lost her divine caste by having given herself to pariahs, to outcasts, and her cheeks kissed by lepers are now covered with a crust of stars. She presses herself against the mangy chests of the camel drivers from the north, who never wash because of the intense cold; she sleeps on vermin-ridden beds with blind beggars; she passes from the embrace of Brahmins to that of miserable creatures, the unclean, whose very presence pollutes the day, who are charged with washing the corpses; and stretched out in the pyramid-shaped shadows of the funeral pyres, Kali abandons herself upon the still warm ashes. She also loves the boatmen, who are rough and strong. She even accepts the black men who work in the bazaar, more harshly beaten than beasts of burden; she rubs her head against their shoulders raw from the swaying of their loads. Wretched as a feverish woman unable to find cool water, she goes from village to village, from crossroads to crossroads, in search of the same mournful delights.

Her tiny feet dance frantically below the chiming anklets, but her eyes never stop weeping, her bitter mouth never kisses, her eyelashes never caress the cheeks of those who embrace her, and her face remains eternally pale like an immaculate moon.

·

A long time ago, Kali, lotus flower of perfection, reigned in Indra's heaven as in the depths of a sapphire; the diamonds of dawn glittered in her eyes, and the universe contracted or expanded in tune with the beatings of her heart.

But Kali, perfect as a flower, ignored her own perfection and, pure as the day itself, had no knowledge of her own purity.

The jealous gods followed Kali one evening, during an eclipse, into a cone of darkness, in a corner of a conniving planet. A bolt of lightning cut her head off. Instead of blood, a torrent of light sprang from her sliced neck. Her halved body, thrown into the abyss by the Jinns, rolled down into the uttermost pit of hell, where those who have not seen or have refused the heavenly light crawl and whimper. A cold wind blew, condensing the clear flakes that started to drop from the sky; a white layer began to collect on the mountaintops, beneath starry spaces where night was falling. The monster gods, the cattle gods, the gods of many arms and many legs like turning wheels, escaped through the shadows, blinded by their halos of fire, and the haggard immortals regretted their crime.

Contrite, the gods descended along the Roof of the World, into the abyss full of smoke where those who once were alive now crawl. They crossed the nine purgatories; they passed prisons of ice and mud, where ghosts devoured by remorse repent the wrongs they have committed, and prisons of fire, where other dead, tormented by vain greed, bemoan the wrongs they did not commit. The gods were astounded to find that man has such an infinite capacity for evil, so many resources and agonies of pleasure and sin. At the bottom of the ossuary, in a swamp, Kali's head bobbed like a water lily, and her long black hair rippled around it like floating roots.

Piously, they picked up the lovely pale head and they set off to find the body that had borne it. A headless body was lying on the shore. They took it, placed Kali's head upon those shoulders, and brought the goddess back to life.

The body was that of a prostitute condemned to death for having sought to trouble the meditations of a young Brahmin. Drained of blood, the ashen corpse seemed pure. The goddess and the harlot had on the left thigh the same beauty spot.

•

Never again did Kali, lotus flower of perfection, reign in Indra's heaven. The body to which the divine head was joined felt homesick for the streets of ill repute, the forbidden encounters, the rooms where the prostitutes, meditating on secret debauches, survey the clients' arrival through the slits of green shutters. She became the seducer of children, the inciter of old men, the ruthless mistress of the young; and the women of the town, neglected by their husbands and feeling like widows, compared Kali's body to the flames of a pyre. She was as unclean as a gutter rat and as loathed as a weasel of the fields. She stole hearts as if they were strips of offal from the butcher's block, and the liquefied fortunes of men clung to her hands like strands of honey. Never resting, from Benares to Kapilavastu, from Bangalore to Srinagar, Kali's body bore the goddess's dishonored head, and her limpid eyes continued to weep.

·

One morning in Benares, Kali, drunk, grimacing with fatigue, left the harlots' street. In the fields, an idiot quietly slobbering, seated at the edge of a dung heap, rose to his feet as she passed and ran after her. When he was barely the length of his shadow away, Kali slowed down and allowed him to overtake her.

After he had left her, she continued her way toward an unknown city. A child begged her for alms, and she did not even warn him that a snake, about to strike, was lifting its head between two stones. She had been overcome by a hatred of all living things, and at the same time by a desire to swell her substance, to annihilate all creatures as she fed on them. She could be seen crouching at the edge of graveyards; her jaws cracked bones like the maw of a lioness. She killed like the female insect devouring the male; she crushed the beings she brought to life like a wild sow turning on her young. Those she killed, she finished off by dancing on their bodies. Her lips stained with blood exuded a dull smell of butcher shops, but her embrace consoled her victims, and the warmth of her breast made them forget all ills.

•

At the edge of a wood, Kali met a wise man.

He was sitting cross-legged, palms placed one against the other, and his wizened body was as dry as firewood. Nobody could have said if he was very young or very old; his all-seeing eyes were barely visible beneath his half-shut lids. Around him the light formed a halo, and Kali felt rising from her own inner depths the presentiment of a vast definitive peace, where worlds would stop and beings would be delivered; of a day of beatitude on which both life and death will be equally useless, an age in which the All will be absorbed into Nothingness, as if that pure vacuity that she had just conceived were quivering within her like a future child.

The Master of Great Compassion lifted a hand to bless the passing woman.

"My immaculate head has been fixed to the body of infamy," she said. "I desire and do not desire, I suffer and yet I enjoy, I loathe living and am afraid to die."

"We are all incomplete," said the wise man. "We are all pieces, fragments, shadows, matterless ghosts.

We all have believed that we have wept and that we have felt pleasure for endless centuries."

"I was a goddess in Indra's heaven," said the harlot.

"And yet you were not freer from the chain of things, nor your diamond body safer from misfortune than your body of flesh and filth. Perhaps, unhappy woman, dishonored traveler of every road, you are about to attain that which has no shape."

"I am tired," moaned the goddess.

Then, touching with the tip of his fingers the black tresses soiled with ashes, he said: "Desire has taught you the emptiness of desire; regret has shown you the uselessness of regret. Be patient, Error of which we are all a part, Imperfect Creature thanks to whom perfection becomes aware of itself, O Lust which is not necessarily immortal . . ."

THE END OF
MARKO KRALJEVIĆ

The bells pealed for the dead in the almost unbearably blue sky. They seemed louder and harsher than elsewhere, as if, in this land bordering the regions of the infidel, they wished to state high and loud that their peals were Christian, and Christian the dead man about to be buried. And yet below, in the white city of narrow yards, where men crouched in the shade, they were heard mingled with cries, shouts, bleating, neighing and braying, and sometimes with whinings of women or their prayers for the recently departed soul, or with the laughter of an idiot who showed no interest in this public mourning. In the brass workers' quarter, the tapping of hammers covered the noise. Old Stevan, who was delicately finishing with light taps the mouth of a pitcher, saw the linen curtain covering the doorway being pulled aside. A little more heat and low afternoon sun seeped into the dark shop.

His friend Andrev entered as if the place were his and sat down cross-legged on a piece of carpet. "Did you know Marko had died? I was there," he said.

"Some customers told me he was dead," the old man answered without laying down his hammer. "As you obviously feel like telling the story, go ahead and tell it while I carry on with my work."

"I have a friend who works in Marko's kitchens.

On holidays, he lets me serve at the table: you can always help yourself to a good piece of something there."

"Today is no holiday," the old man said, caressing the copper lip.

"No, but you always eat well at Marko's, even on working days, and even on the days when the Church forbids us to eat meat. And there are always many people at the table: mainly crippled old men, who never stop talking about their fine exploits in Kosovo. But fewer and fewer of them come every year, even from season to season. And today Marko had also invited powerful merchants, village elders who live in the mountains, so close to the Turks that they can shoot arrows at each other across the stream, and in the summer, when the water is low, it flows with blood. The dinner was in honor of their annual expedition to bring back Turkish cattle and donkeys. Huge dishes were served in which no spices were spared; the platters were heavy, and slippery to hold because of the grease. Marko ate and drank like ten hungry men, and talked more than he ate, and laughed and banged his fist more than he drank. And from time to time he would put an end to the men's quarrels, when two of them fought with an eye on the forthcoming loot.

"And after we, the waiters, had poured water

over all the hands and wiped all the fingers, he came out into the large courtyard full of people. In town they know that the leftovers are distributed to whoever wants them, and the rest is thrown to the dogs. Most people bring along a pot, small or large, or a bowl, or at least a basket. Marko knew almost all of them. There was no one like him for remembering names and faces, and for giving the right face its proper name. To a man on crutches he spoke of the time they had fought together against the Bey Constantine; to a blind sitar player he hummed the first line of a ballad the man had written in his honor when he was young; and taking an ugly old woman by the chin, he reminded her of the good old times when they had slept together. And sometimes he himself would take a piece of lamb from a dish and say to someone: 'Eat!' It was just like any other day.

"But then, suddenly, Marko came upon a little old man sitting on a bench, with his feet dangling in front of him.

" 'And you,' he said, 'why have you not brought your bowl? I cannot remember your name.'

" 'Some call me this, some call me that,' said the little old man. 'It does not matter.'

" 'I do not recall your face either,' said Marko. 'Perhaps because you look like everyone else. I am not fond of strangers, or of beggars who do not beg. And if by chance you were spying for the Turks?'

" 'Some say I am always spying,' the old man said. 'But they are mistaken: I let people do as they please.'

" 'I, too, like to do as I please,' shouted Marko. 'Your face doesn't agree with me. Leave at once!'

"And he caught him with his foot, to topple him from the bench. But the old man seemed made of stone. Or rather, no: he did not appear more solid than anyone else; his sandaled feet still dangled in front of him, and no one would have said that Marko had touched him.

"And when Marko grabbed him by the shoulders to make him rise, the same thing happened. The old man wagged his head.

" 'Get up and fight like a man,' Marko cried, all red in the face.

"The little old man rose. He was very small: he barely reached Marko's shoulder. He stood there not doing or saying anything. Marko fell on him, clenching his fists. But it seemed as if his blows never reached the old man, and yet Marko's knuckles were all bloody.

" 'You there,' Marko cried to his guard, 'keep out of this. This concerns only myself.'

"But his breath was short. Suddenly he stumbled

and fell heavily on the ground. I swear the old man had not moved.

"'That was a bad fall, Marko,' he said. 'You shall not rise again. I think you knew as much even before you began.'

"But there is that expedition against the Turks which I have organized: it is, as it were, all set to go,' the man on the ground said painfully. 'And yet what must be must be.'

"'Against the Turks, or for them?' asked the little old man. 'You know you sometimes crossed from one side to the other.'

"'The girl I was courting, and who hinted as much,' said the dying man, 'had her right arm cut off by me. And there were those prisoners I beheaded in spite of my promises . . . But after all, there aren't only evil deeds to be taken into account. I gave to the priests, I gave to the poor . . .'

"'Do not start to make your accounts,' said the old man. 'It is always too early or too late, and always useless. Rather, allow me to place my jacket under your head, to make you more comfortable on the ground.'

"He took off his jacket and did as he had said. We were all too astounded to stop him. And also, come to think of it, there was nothing he had really done. He walked toward the doors, which were wide open. With his back somewhat arched, he seemed, even more than before, a beggar, but a beggar who asked for nothing. Two dogs were chained to the doorway; as he walked by, he put his hand on ferocious Big Black's head. Big Black did not bare his teeth. Now that we knew Marko was dead, we all turned our heads toward the doorway to watch the old man leave. Outside, as you know, the road stretches straight between two hills, first rising, then descending, finally rising again. He was already quite far away. You could see someone walking on the dusty road, dragging his feet a little, with his baggy trousers flapping against his thighs and his shirt billowing in the wind. For an old man, he walked quickly. And above his head, in the otherwise empty sky, a flock of wild geese was flying."

THE SADNESS OF
CORNELIUS BERG

Since his arrival in Amsterdam, Cornelius Berg had taken up lodgings at several inns. He changed inns frequently, moving when it was time to pay, sometimes still painting small portraits, commissioned pictures on a set theme, and, here and there, a nude for a private collection, as well as begging along the streets for the alms of a shop sign to paint. Unfortunately, his hand trembled; he was forced to use thicker and thicker lenses in his spectacles. Whatever steadiness his hand still possessed had been wasted away by tobacco, and wine, for which he had acquired a taste in Italy. He grew to abhor his work, refused to deliver it, spoiled everything he did by overlaying and scratching out, and ended by simply not working.

He would spend long hours deep inside taverns as smoky as a drunkard's conscience, where old disciples of Rembrandt's, his fellow students of long ago, would pay for his drink, hoping that he would tell them of his travels. But the lands dusty with sun through which Cornelius had dragged his brushes and pots of color turned out to be less clear in his memory than they had been in his dreams of travel; and he no longer found it easy, as he had in his youth, to tell rude tales that made the servant girls cluck with laughter. Those who remembered the boisterous Cornelius of the past were surprised to find him so taciturn; only the wine restored his speech, and even then his words were incomprehensible. He would sit, his face turned toward the wall, his hat drawn over his eyes, so as not to see the public, which, he said, disgusted him. All his life, Cornelius, old portrait painter, long ago established in a garret in Rome, had carefully observed the human face; now he turned away from it with irritation or indifference; he went so far as to say that he did not like painting animals, because they were too similar to people.

As he lost the little talent he had ever possessed, genius seemed to come to him instead. He would stand in front of his easel in his untidy attic and place by his side a beautiful, rare, and expensive fruit, which he would hasten to reproduce on the canvas before its lustrous skin lost its freshness, or sometimes even a simple pot, or vegetable peels. A yellowish light filled the room; the rain humbly washed the windows; there was dampness everywhere. The humidity turned into liquid and bloated the rugged sphere of the orange; soaked into the woodwork, which creaked a little; tarnished the copper of the pot. But soon he would lay down his brushes; his stiff fingers, so ready in days gone by to paint on command recumbent Venuses and blond-bearded Christs blessing naked children and draped women, refused to reproduce on the canvas that double flow of dampness and diffused light, which impregnated all things and soaked the sky. His deformed hands, when touching the objects he no longer painted, were all tenderness. In the melancholy Amsterdam street, he dreamed of fields shivering with dew, lovelier than the banks of the dusky Anio, but deserted, too holy for man. This old man, bloated with poverty, seemed to suffer from hydropsy of the heart. Cornelius Berg, polishing off here and there some pitiful work, was in his dreams like Rembrandt himself.

He had not kept in touch with whatever family he still had. A few of his relatives failed to recognize him; others pretended not to know him. The only one who still greeted him was the old syndic of Haarlem.

Throughout a whole spring he worked in that clean, clear city, where he was employed to paint imitation wood carvings on the church wall. In the evening, once his task was over, he would, not unwillingly, visit the old man, who lived alone, turned gently stupid by an uneventful existence, in the sugary care of a maid, and who knew nothing about art. Cornelius would push open the flimsy gate of painted wood; in the small garden, near the canal, the tulip lover would be waiting for him among the flowers. Those priceless bulbs meant nothing to Cornelius, but he could cleverly distinguish even the smallest details in their shapes, the faintest hues in their colors, and he knew that the old syndic invited him only to ask his opinion about a new variety. No one could have found words to describe the infinite diversity of whites, blues, pinks, and mauves. Slender, rigid, the patrician chalices grew from the rich, dark soil: a damp odor, rising from the earth, floated untainted above the perfumeless blooms. The old syndic would balance a pot on his knees, and holding a stem between two fingers, as if by the waist, would, without saying anything, invite Cornelius to admire the delicate marvel. They exchanged few words; Cornelius Berg would give his opinion by nodding his head.

On that day, the syndic was pleased with an achievement even rarer than his previous ones: the flower, white and purple, was striped almost like an iris. He observed it closely, turning it in every direction, and, setting it down by his feet, said: "God is a great painter."

Cornelius Berg did not answer. The quiet old man went on: "God is the painter of the universe."

Cornelius Berg was staring at both the flower and the canal. The tarnished lead mirror reflected nothing but flower beds, brick walls, and the washer-women's washing, but the old tired wanderer could vaguely see in it his own life. He could see certain features of faces observed during his long voyages, the sordid Orient, the untidy south, expressions of greed, of stupidity or fierceness glimpsed under so many beautiful skies; the miserable dwellings, the shameful diseases, the knife-fed brawls on the thresholds of taverns, the wizened faces of money-lenders, and the lovely body of his model Frédérique Gerritsdochter, stretched out on the anatomy table of the Medical School in Freiburg. Then another memory came to him. In Constantinople, where he had painted a number of sultans' portraits for the ambassador of the United Provinces, he had once admired another tulip garden, the pride and joy of a pasha who trusted the painter to immortalize, in its brief perfection, his floral harem. Inside a marble courtyard, the assembled tulips seemed to quiver and rustle, with soft or striking colors. Over a pond a bird was singing; the tips of the cypresses pierced the pale blue sky. But the slave who, following his master's orders, showed these marvels to the stranger was blind in one eye, and the recently emptied socket swarmed with flies.

Taking off his glasses, Cornelius echoed: "God is the painter of the universe."

And then bitterly, in a low voice: "What a shame, Mr. Syndic, that God should not have limited himself to painting landscapes."

POSTSCRIPT

This edition of *Oriental Tales*, in spite of very many purely stylistic corrections, leaves the tales essentially as they were when they appeared for the first time in bookstores in 1938. Only the ending of the story called "Kali Beheaded" was rewritten, to better emphasize certain metaphysical concepts from which this legend is inseparable, and without which, told in a Western manner, it is nothing but a vague erotic tale placed in an Indian setting. Another story, "The Prisoners of the Kremlin," a very early effort to reinterpret in a modern way an ancient Slavic legend, has been omitted as too obviously unworthy to merit repairs.

Of the ten remaining stories (*Tales and Stories* would perhaps have been a better title in view of the varied material), four are transcriptions, more or less freely developed by myself, of authentic fables and legends. "How Wang-Fo Was Saved" is based on a Taoist fable of ancient China; "Marko's Smile" and "The Milk of Death" are taken from Balkan ballads of the Middle Ages; "Kali Beheaded" was inspired by an inexhaustible Hindu myth, the same that, interpreted in an entirely different manner, provided Goethe with "The God and the Bayadere" and Thomas Mann with *The Transposed Heads*. On the other hand, "The Man Who Loved the Nereids" and "Aphrodissia, the Widow" (originally called "The Red Chief" and retitled to avoid political overtones) have, as their starting point, different events or superstitions from present-day Greece, or rather the Greece of yesterday, since they were written between 1932 and 1937. "Our-Lady-of-the-Swallows," on the contrary, is a personal fantasy of the author, born of the wish to explain the charming name of a small chapel in the Attic countryside. In "The Last Love of Prince Genji," the characters and setting of the story are borrowed, not from a myth or a legend, but from a great literary text of the past, the remarkable eleventh-century Japanese novel *Genji Monogatari* by the Lady Murasaki Shikibu, which tells, in six or seven volumes, the adventures of a subtle and refined Asian Don Juan. But, because of a characteristic Japanese artistic delicacy, Murasaki passes over her hero's death and moves from a chapter in which Genji, now a widower, decides to retire from the world to a chapter in which his death has already taken place. The intention of the story you have just read is, if not to fill the gap, at least to imagine what his death might have been like had Murasaki herself composed it. "The End of Marko Kraljević" is a story I had been wanting to write for many years and finally completed in 1978. The inspiration for this tale was a fragment of a Serbian ballad on the death of the hero at the hands of a mysterious, unprepossessing, allegorical stranger. But where did

I read or hear this story, about which I have so often thought? I no longer know, and I cannot find it among the several books on the subject I have at hand, which give many different versions of Marko Kraljević's death, but not this one. Finally, "The Sadness of Cornelius Berg" ("Cornelius Berg's Tulips," in the earliest version) was conceived as the conclusion of a novel that remains unfinished. Not in the least Oriental, except for a couple of brief allusions to the artist's travels in Asia Minor (and one of these is a recent addition), this story does not really belong in this collection. But I could not resist the idea of placing, opposite the great Chinese painter, lost and saved within his own work, this obscure contemporary of Rembrandt's, sadly meditating on his own accomplishments.

May I remind those readers interested in bibliography that "Kali Beheaded" first appeared in *La Revue Européenne* in 1928; "Wang-Fo" and "Genji," respectively, in *La Revue de Paris* in 1936 and 1937; and during those same years—1936 and 1937—"Marko's Smile" and "The Milk of Death" in *Les Nouvelles Littéraires*, and "The Man Who Loved the Nereids" in *La Revue de France*. "The End of Marko Kraljević" appeared in *La Nouvelle Revue Française* in 1978.

M.Y.